I0953382

# THE VISCONTI HOUSE

# THE VISCONTI  HOUSE

## ELSBETH EDGAR

CANDLEWICK PRESS

Copyright © 2011 by Elsbeth Edgar

First U.S. edition 2011

Library of Congress Cataloging-in-Publication Data is available.

Library of Congress Catalog Card Number pending

ISBN 978-0-7636-5019-3

10 11 12 13 14 15 RRC 10 9 8 7 6 5 4 3 2 1

Printed in Crawfordsville, IN, U.S.A.

This book was typeset in Caslon 540.

Candlewick Press
99 Dover Street
Somerville, Massachusetts 02144

visit us at www.candlewick.com

*For Jonathan, Katherine, and Elizabeth*

# ← CHAPTER 1 →

Laura's alarm was ringing, the shrill sound reverberating through the empty corners of her room. Laura did not stir. It was Monday—there was nothing to stir for. Yesterday her alarm had not rung, but she had been up before dawn. In the cold, gray light she had pulled her comforter around her shoulders and written in a glorious frenzy of inspiration until her cat, Samson, had strolled in, mewing for breakfast. Then she had put on several sweaters and gone out into the old orchard to watch the sun rise.

But that was yesterday. Today she had to go back to school.

Today vacation was over.

"Laura!"

Laura opened one eye. Her father was standing in the doorway, tying up his old checked bathrobe. There were shadows under his eyes, and his voice was tired.

"Turn off the alarm. It's time to get up."

"I don't want to get up. I don't want to move." Laura buried herself beneath the bedcovers and closed her eyes tightly. She heard her father crossing the room. Before she had time to get a firm grip on the comforter, however, he had whipped it off.

"Let us, then, be up and doing," he declaimed, waving the comforter in the air.

"With a heart for any fate;

Still achieving, still pursuing,

Learn to labor and to wait."

Laura groaned. "I don't want to labor," she muttered, rolling off the bed.

Her father dropped the comforter onto the floor. "Neither do I," he replied, his voice tired again. "But I have an article to finish, and you have things to learn."

Laura scowled at him and headed for the door. Other people didn't have fathers who quoted poetry at them first thing in the morning, she thought as she stumbled down the long hallway to the bathroom. Their fathers probably never quoted poetry at them at all. And if they did, it would be some silly little rhyme, not Longfellow. Most fathers had probably never heard of Longfellow.

She grimaced at her reflection in the mirror, trying to flatten the unruly curls that fell over her forehead. None of the other girls at school had curls like that. Their hair was long and straight, and their eyebrows—Laura leaned forward, staring at her own dejectedly—were fine and shaped, not thick and dark. Other people were normal and had normal families; they did ordinary things and lived in ordinary houses. Laura felt tears welling in her eyes. If only they were back in Melbourne, snug in their little row house. Nobody had stared at her there. Nobody had called her weird. She squeezed out her soap and started scrubbing her face, wishing she could scrub away all that difference.

When she came into the kitchen, her father was slumped at the table, cradling a cup of coffee in his hands. He had been working late into the night again—she had seen the light glowing in the study when Samson had woken her at three in the morning, wanting to play. She felt a twinge of guilt for making her father get up. Journalists always had deadlines to meet, but now that he was freelance, her father seemed to have to work so much harder than before.

"It's all right; you can go back to bed," she said, pouring some muesli into a bowl.

"Sadly, I can't. The article is due this afternoon. If you're sure you're awake, I'll get back to it."

"I'm sure." Laura opened the fridge and took out the milk, sniffing it to make sure it was not rancid. It often was.

"You're not going to sneak back to your room?" her father persisted, rising.

She made a face at him. "Of course not!"

After he had left, she wandered over to the window and stood staring at the wild rosebushes outside as she ate, wishing forlornly that it was Saturday again and not Monday. Wishing that it was the beginning of vacation, not the end. Wishing that something terrible (but not *too* terrible) had happened and that the school had been closed for a long time, possibly forever, and that she would never have to go back.

When she had finished her breakfast, she crept into her parents' bedroom and climbed onto the bed beside her mother. "I don't want to go to school," she said.

Her mother reached out an arm and drew her under the blankets, shoes and all. "Why not?"

Laura snuggled into the bed. "I want to stay home with you."

"I'm sorry, honey bear—that's not possible."

Laura squirmed down farther, her head almost buried under the covers. "Some people don't go to school. They do their lessons at home."

Her mother stroked her hair softly. "That's because they have very clever parents who can teach them math and science."

"I don't want to learn math and science."

"Yes, you do. You just don't know it yet."

"I don't! And you can teach me writing and art and geography and history."

"Not well enough."

Laura gave a little snort and burrowed deeper still into the bed, until her head was completely covered. She could feel the warm darkness seeping through her, blotting out the morning. If only she could stay there, hidden and protected, for the rest of the day.

"Aha. Caught!" Her father suddenly pulled back the blankets. "It's time for you to leave. I knew you were planning to slip back to bed."

"I was not!" she retorted. "It just happened." She did not move, however.

Her mother sat up and reached for the clock. "It's a quarter past eight. If you don't leave now, you'll be late."

Laura pictured Miss Grisham standing by the

office, handing out late passes. The image was chilling. Miss Grisham was her least favorite teacher; she always looked at Laura suspiciously, even though Laura never did anything wrong. The thought of having to approach her made Laura scramble off the bed. She collected her bag, called a reproachful good-bye to her parents, and pushed open the kitchen door.

The garden was shining in the morning light. Enormous pink flowers covered the sprawling hydrangea bushes down the side of the house and, around the front, the red camellias were still blooming beside the stone steps, their petals bright against the glossy green leaves. The garden called invitingly, as did the old orchard behind the house, about to burst into leaf. Laura looked toward her tree house nestled in the branches of an old apple tree, then turned and clumped along the driveway to the huge cast-iron gates, stopping briefly to glance back at the house before setting off down the hill toward the high school. Behind her, she could feel the imposing facade looming in all its shabby grandeur.

The first time Laura had seen the house, she thought it was enchanted. Looking up at the long elegant windows, with their small balconies and intricate wrought-iron decoration, she thought she had never seen anything so beautiful. She couldn't believe that they were going to live in such a fairy-tale world. Everything had been exciting then: moving to the country, finding the house, her parents quitting their jobs. "We are going to live in a castle and follow our dreams," her mother had said.

But it hadn't turned out like that. Not for Laura, anyway. She looked out over the town, spreading before her, brown and dry. The houses were all modest, sensible houses with modest, sensible gardens. Not like hers, she thought, not at all like hers. And the people in them were modest, sensible people who had lived there all their lives. Not like her. Not at all like her.

She glanced at her watch and began to walk faster. The train tracks ran through the town, crossing the road at the bottom of the hill and passing a small weatherboard house with a vegetable garden in the front yard. As always, Laura scanned the garden to see if Mrs. Murphy was outside, watering her plants.

Mrs. Murphy was the only other person in town who was different—as far as Laura could tell. But she was not different like Laura's family was different. She wore socks instead of stockings and cardigans over cotton dresses, even in winter, and sometimes muttered to herself while she worked. Laura always said hello to her because she thought that she should, but she never stopped. She already felt isolated enough; she did not want to be known as the girl who talked to Mrs. Murphy. Today there was no sign of her, thankfully, and Laura breathed a sigh of relief.

Then she hesitated. Something had caught her eye. A movement, nothing more, but it did not seem like Mrs. Murphy. Laura squinted. Someone had come out the back door and was putting trash in a can.

A boy.

Laura stared. What could a boy be doing at Mrs. Murphy's house? She had never seen anyone else there before. Ever. She watched him stop, look idly around, and then wander back inside. Strange, she thought, as she shifted her bag to her other shoulder and continued on.

A group of older boys was hanging around the gate when she arrived at school, their bags blocking the path. With a sinking heart, Laura recognized them as the kids who hung around the bike shed, smoking. For a moment she considered hurrying on to another gate but realized that she would have to pass them anyway. She looked around anxiously for someone she knew, but no one was in sight.

One of the boys nudged another and jerked his head in her direction. "Here comes the kid from the haunted house," he jeered. "Seen any dead people lately?"

The others started laughing, and Laura hurried by. When she reached the locker room, she was relieved to find Janie Middleton and Kylie Jackson unpacking their books. She smiled at the girls and walked into class behind them, feeling almost as if she was one of their group.

"Have you finished the math homework?" asked Kylie as they all sat down.

Laura nodded.

"It was hard, wasn't it?" Kylie frowned as she unzipped her pencil case and began arranging her pens on the desk.

Laura nodded again. Actually, she had found it easy, but she was not going to say that out loud—not when she knew that Kylie Jackson had found it difficult.

Mr. Parker strode into the room, a pile of papers under his arm, his bicycle clips still clamped to his legs. Without waiting for the stragglers to take their seats, he began handing out work sheets. "I suggest you begin right away," he said. "I'll be collecting these at the end of class. Those who haven't finished can see me at lunchtime to explain why."

Laura finished early and was gazing out the window, her chin cupped in her hands, dreaming of the dragon book she was writing, when Mr. Jameson, the principal, came into the room. He was followed by a tall boy in oversize shorts and a too-small sweater. The boy glared defiantly at the class, and they looked warily back at him, taking in his roughly cut hair and the way his fists were clenched by his side.

"This is Leon Murphy," said Mr. Jameson. "He'll be joining 8A. I am sure you will make him welcome." Kylie giggled, and Mr. Parker fixed her with an angry frown.

*That's the boy I saw,* thought Laura, staring. He must be Mrs. Murphy's grandson—but why would he be staying with her? At that moment his eyes flicked over her, and she felt her face redden. Furious with herself, she looked away to the patch of blue sky she had been dreaming in just a minute ago.

"Leon, come and sit down here next to Peter," she heard Mr. Parker say as Mr. Jameson left the room.

"Peter, I want you to look after Leon and show him around."

There was an undercurrent of stifled laughter, and the boy behind Peter poked him. "I can't, sir," said Peter. "I've got soccer practice at lunchtime."

"Mike, then." Mr. Parker turned to a large boy who was busily working on his assignment. Mike jumped. He opened his mouth, then closed it, nodded, and went back to his work. The boys in the back row sniggered again, and when Mike reluctantly led Leon from the room at the end of class, one of them called out, "Fatso and Skinnybones." Mike flushed, but Leon just continued walking as though he had not heard.

Leon was ahead of Laura when she came through the gate after school. He was running his hand along the fences, his shoulders slightly hunched. Laura slowed her steps so that she would not overtake him, and when she arrived at Mrs. Murphy's house, he was already inside.

The front door was open, however, for the first time that she could remember. Looking down the dark hallway, she saw a heavy curtain hanging in the middle and shivered, wondering what was behind it.

## ✦ CHAPTER 2 ✦

The next day Laura noticed that Leon was no longer walking around with Mike. He was not walking around with anyone. In class he sat alone, and during recess and lunch he sat outside the bike shed and read. She was not the only one who was aware of Leon's behavior. While they were changing for gym, it was all that Kylie and Maddy Patterson could talk about.

"Did you hear?" Maddy whispered as she pulled her gym clothes out of her bag. "Leon Murphy's father is a criminal. I bet that's why he had to move here."

"No." Kylie's eyes widened with curiosity. "What do you think he did?"

"Killed someone, I bet. Leon Murphy looks like he has a father who killed someone, doesn't he?"

"I don't know. What does that look like?"

"Leon Murphy!" They both started giggling.

"Girls!" Miss Stevenson called sharply from the door.

Although she had not been part of the conversation, Laura felt as though she, too, had been rebuked. How did they know about Leon's father, anyway? She grabbed her sneakers and pulled them on, looking over at Maddy's long legs and wishing that hers were lean and tanned, too. She lifted her head and was engulfed in Kylie's spray-on deodorant. The scented mist was everywhere, making her cough and feel slightly sick.

"Sorry," said Kylie, and she started giggling again.

Laura hurried outside, wondering what it would be like to find everything so amusing all the time. She looked back at Kylie and Maddy, sitting together on the bench. They never seemed to worry about anything.

"Twice around the oval and then back here for basketball drills," shouted Miss Stevenson. "Hurry up, now — get a move on."

Laura groaned and began moving slowly toward the sports fields.

"Running, Laura," Miss Stevenson called after her. "Not daydreaming. You should be halfway around by now."

Laura broke into a reluctant jog, her thoughts jolting around her head in a mantra of discontent. *If only I didn't have to go to school. If only I could just stay home. If only I didn't have to go to school.* She looked up and saw Leon, sitting alone under a tree. *How come he doesn't have to run? It's so unfair.* The mantra began again. *If only I didn't have to go to school.*

As if everything wasn't bad enough, Miss Stevenson asked her to return the equipment to the staff room after gym. It was the last class, and by the time she was crossing the school yard, her bag heavy on her back, almost everyone had gone. She remembered the cheerful bustle of her old school, with all the parents and students milling around after the last bell. The only sounds she could hear now were the harsh cries of the galahs circling overhead and the soccer team training on the oval in the distance.

Laura headed home, walking quickly, absorbed in her sense of injustice, her eyes fixed on the sidewalk, until the sound of approaching footsteps made her turn. Shocked, she saw Leon Murphy coming up behind her, limping. His shirt was torn, and his left eye was swelling. He shot her a hostile look as he passed and, for a moment, all Laura could think of was the conversation she had overheard. Could it have been true? Was his father a criminal, and was Leon just like his father? She looked around nervously. There was no one nearby.

Then Leon stumbled. He leaned over to catch his breath, and at once Laura felt ashamed of her suspicions. She hesitated, wondering what to do. He probably wouldn't want her to do anything, but he looked as though he was really hurt.

"Are you OK?" she asked. Leon did not reply, so she repeated the question, a little louder this time.

Leon bit his lip and straightened up. "I'm fine."

"What happened?"

"Nothing." Laura stood peering at him, and he snapped. "I'm all right; you don't have to stare at me. You can go. And you don't need to feel sorry for me, either."

"I don't." Laura averted her eyes from the cut on his forehead, which was oozing blood.

"I'm all right."

"I can see that."

"I am!" He glared at her, then shrugged and began to hobble on.

"So what happened?" she repeated, falling into step beside him.

"It was just some kids at school. It was nothing. I shouldn't have gotten involved."

"What did they do?"

Leon looked at her, his gaze measuring. "They took

my book. They took my book and threw it around." He paused, still watching her. "It was my father's book," he said at last, and continued walking.

Laura felt her mouth drop open, and she quickly closed it. That was the last thing she had expected. "Did you get it back?" she asked, hurrying after him.

"Yes."

There was something in the way Leon said this that made Laura think the kids would not take his things again. She suspected that Leon was not the only one with a black eye. "How many were there?"

"Four." They had reached the crossing at the dip in the road. Mrs. Murphy's house was on the other side. "I gotta go," he said. "Keep this to yourself, OK?"

"Of course," replied Laura.

Leon pushed the gate open and was halfway down the path when Laura realized that she had not asked the most important question. "Is it all right?" she called after him.

He looked back at her, puzzled. "What?"

"The book. Is it all right?"

Leon's eyes darkened. "It's torn," he said, his voice suddenly trembling with anger. "They tore my father's book. I hate them. I hate them all."

He disappeared around the back of the house,

and Laura braced herself for the sound of a door slamming.

It didn't come. Leon closed the door very gently.

The hill to her house usually seemed steep to Laura at the end of the day. This afternoon, however, she was almost at the top before she realized it. Her mind was focused on Leon and his father and the book. She felt as though they were all parts of a pattern that she couldn't fit together—and she wasn't sure that she wanted to. In fact, the more she thought about it, the more she was sure that she didn't. Laura didn't want anything to do with Leon Murphy.

She looked up at the heavy iron gates in front of her and breathed a sigh of relief. Once she was through those gates, she would be safe. Then she could forget—forget about school and the town and Leon Murphy. Particularly about Leon Murphy.

It was overcast, and the lights were on in her mother's studio. They shone through the dark leaves of the rosebushes, warm and inviting. Laura crunched down the gravel path and pushed open the door to the kitchen. It was empty and filled with shadows. Piles of newspapers covered the table, and the smell of stale coffee hung in the air.

It was also cold. They had no central heating, just the huge fireplaces in the cavernous rooms and two little space heaters that they had bought. "This is Australia," her father always said as she and her mother huddled around the heaters. "We don't need central heating." He said this even when the wind was slipping under the windows and the rain was beating against them. Laura knew that he said it because heating would cost too much to install. Now that her parents didn't have permanent jobs, they were always having to think about money.

She grabbed an apple from the bowl on the tall sideboard and continued through to the studio. This was the largest and grandest room in the house. It had once been a ballroom, and the old oak floorboards were still there, as were the ornate patterns in the plaster ceiling. The elaborate paintwork had long since gone, however, and so had the velvet curtains and candelabra.

Now it was filled with chunks of stone and metal. It was where her mother worked. It was also where they all relaxed and entertained and where, curled up on the sofa at one end, Laura did most of her homework. Laura was always finding corners in the vast rooms where she could make a small space of her own.

"Hello, honey bear. Was today as bad as you expected?" Her mother blew her a kiss and continued to chisel the large piece of stone in front of her.

"Yes," replied Laura. She dumped her bag by the window and slumped onto the sofa, drawing a knitted blanket around her. It smelled of comfort and home.

"Well, here's some good news to cheer you up. Harry just called. He's coming to visit."

Laura immediately brightened. She liked Harry, and it was always fun when he was there. "When?"

"Next month, for the long weekend. And he's bringing a friend."

"Oh." Laura wasn't sure if this was good news or not. Some of the people Harry knew were very strange. "What sort of friend?"

"I don't know. Some sort of singer, I think. Or an actor? I don't remember." Her mother frowned, running her hand down the rough stone. "Do you think I've gone in too deeply here?"

"No. Tell me more about the singer."

"I don't know any more. He just said she was a singer—I think."

"She!" Laura bit into the apple thoughtfully. Harry had never brought a woman to stay before. "Well, I just hope she's not like that poet who walked around in a top hat and jester's boots." She giggled. "Or that philosopher who kept telling us the world was about to end."

"Yes, he was a little trying," agreed her mother, smiling. "But I'm sure Isabella will be very nice. Do you mind if we don't eat for a while? I just want to finish this section before dinner."

"Mom, we always eat late," said Laura as she started dragging her schoolbooks from her bag. "But it's all right. I don't mind."

And she didn't. When she was at home, everything was fine.

# ← CHAPTER 3 →

Laura's suspicions were correct; two other boys at school did have bruises. Leon went about his work as though nothing had happened. He hardly seemed aware of his discolored face or the bandage across his forehead. He did not look at Laura, nor she at him. Everyone was talking about the fight, of course. At recess Laura stood around with Kylie, Janie, and Maddy and was reluctantly drawn into their conversation.

"They say he went crazy. It was George and Pete from 9D—that group. They were just teasing. They tried to get a look at the book he was reading, and he went mental." Kylie's eyes grew large as she spoke. "He started shouting at them and throwing punches. Really crazy stuff. As if it matters, anyway. It was just a book; it wasn't even new."

Laura dug the ground with the tip of her shoe, not looking at them.

"He lives near you, doesn't he?" said Janie,

turning to her. "You'd better be careful. He might come prowling at night. I bet he steals things, like his dad. He probably stole that old book."

Laura shifted her feet and glanced around, hoping Leon wasn't nearby. Fortunately, he was nowhere in sight.

"Laura will be all right." Maddy giggled. "She'll be protected by her ghosts."

"I don't have any ghosts," protested Laura.

The others laughed. "Everyone knows your house is haunted," said Kylie. "It must be so weird living there." She raised her arms, pretending to lunge at Laura and making a silly "Ooooh" sound. Maddy and Janie cowered in mock terror.

Laura managed a tiny smile, but inside she felt completely dispirited. Why did everyone always make fun of her house? It was just a house. A beautiful, old house. She looked at the girls, wondering if they could ever comprehend that.

"So what's it like, living in a mansion?" asked Maddy.

Laura heard the bell ring and breathed a sigh of relief. "We should go," she said. "You know how annoyed Mr. Parker gets if we're late." She began hurrying toward the locker room, not looking at

Maddy. Laura never talked about her parents or her home, and she never asked anyone to visit. She always pretended that her mother could cook and was strict about bedtimes and worried about mud on the floor—just like other mothers. She pretended that her father was interested in soccer and got cross if she didn't do her homework—just like other fathers. She never mentioned the huge blocks of stone that arrived from the quarry and were heaved through the French windows into the ballroom or the reams of paper that lay in dusty piles around her father's study.

Laura pretended a lot of things. But she couldn't pretend about her house. Everyone knew it was different. It was not a weatherboard cottage or a neat brick veneer; it was a grand, old, crumbling Italianate villa, surrounded by a tangle of dying fruit trees and overgrown roses, rising in faded splendor above the town. It was the sort of house that people like Kylie and Maddy and Janie would never understand.

As she trailed into math class, she noticed that Mr. Parker was carrying a pile of printed sheets. "A surprise test," he announced. "To see if anyone has been listening to what I say every day."

There was an immediate uproar, but Mr. Parker remained unmoved. "This is a state competition, but

I want you to use it as a way of working out what you know. I don't expect you to find it easy, so don't panic if there are some questions you can't do."

The test was long and hard, and most people were still writing when the bell rang at the end of class. Even Laura found it difficult. At one point she looked across the room and saw that Leon had stopped writing altogether. She felt a stab of pity, guessing that he probably didn't have a clue what to do.

The following day, when Mr. Parker asked Leon to stay after class, she was sure he must have done really badly. Apparently, everyone else thought so, too, as they sniggered and whispered to one another. Leon said nothing, but the next math class he was not there and Laura supposed he must be doing remedial work. She wondered if it would help, hoping vaguely that it would.

Over the next week, Laura often saw Leon ahead of her, walking quickly as though, like her, he was trying to escape. If he was not too far ahead, he would half nod to her as he turned in to Mrs. Murphy's garden. Laura would half nod back, but she tried to pace her steps so that he would have gone in before she arrived.

"So do you ever speak to Leon Murphy?" asked

Kylie one morning as they stood at their lockers, taking out their books.

"Of course not." Laura glanced at her. Why would Kylie suppose that?

Kylie shoved her bag into her locker and slammed the door before it could fall out. She turned to Laura. "What do you think he does at old Mrs. Murphy's?"

Laura shook her head. "I don't know. Why are you so interested?"

"I'm not. I just think it's strange that he's there, that's all. I mean, why did he come to stay with his grandmother? Why isn't he with his mother, wherever she is? What is he doing here?" Kylie tossed back her hair and contemplated Laura. "You must see him around. You go past his house every day. You must see something."

Laura felt her face redden. "I don't see anything," she replied, hugging her books to her chest. "Anyway, I'm not thinking about Leon Murphy when I'm walking home."

"What *are* you thinking about, then?" Kylie was watching her curiously.

*Dragons*, thought Laura, but said, "Nothing. Nothing much." Laura was thinking about dragons because of the book she was writing and illustrating. It was about different dragon species. Every afternoon, as soon as she had finished her homework (and sometimes before), she would curl up in her corner of the studio and work on it. The dragons were so real to her that some evenings she thought she could almost see them flying though the dusk with their beautiful fragile wings and their funny fiery snouts. This was not something that she was going to talk about with Kylie, however. Like her house and her family, Laura never mentioned her writing to anyone at school.

"You're strange, Laura Horton." Kylie shrugged and started moving toward the door. "If I was walking past Leon's house every day, I'd be trying to find out everything I could about him. Maybe I should be a detective when I leave school. I bet I'd be good at it." She caught sight of Maddy in the distance. "See you," she called, and dashed off, leaving Laura alone in the corridor.

Laura slammed her locker shut. If only there were other kids at school like her. Just one would be enough. Someone she could talk to. Someone who would catch sight of her and call out and want to be with her.

She sighed. As if that was going to happen. There

was no one like her. As everyone kept telling her, she was strange.

The Friday before the long weekend, the whole school squashed into the auditorium for an unexpected assembly. From where she sat, Laura could see Leon lounging in his seat. She tried to imagine how he was going to spend the next three days. Would he go back to his parents, wherever they were? To his father, whose books he defended so passionately? To his mother? Or would he be staying with Mrs. Murphy? The thought of being shut up in that little white house by the train tracks made Laura shudder.

A hush fell as the principal rose and looked out across the student body. "I have an exciting announcement to make," he began. Everyone stopped fidgeting in their seats and waited. "We have the results of a competition the Year Eight students participated in a few weeks ago."

Laura stiffened. She had forgotten about that. She hoped she was not going to be called out again.

"We have an outstanding achievement," Mr. Jameson continued. "One of our students has won one of the top prizes."

Laura relaxed. It couldn't be her. She was good at math but not that good, and she knew she had made mistakes. Her mind whirled, trying to think who it could be.

"Leon Murphy," said the principal.

A gasp rippled through the hall, and Laura did a complete double take. Leon Murphy wasn't struggling after all. He was bright. Really bright!

She watched as he got slowly to his feet and began walking toward the stage. He did not look particularly pleased. In fact, he did not look pleased at all. His expression, as he stood glowering at the assembled school, reminded Laura of a caged wildcat.

As soon as they were dismissed, Leon shouldered his way through the crowd and headed for the exit. By the time Laura had collected her bag and was leaving the school grounds, he was a tiny figure disappearing down the hill ahead of her.

## CHAPTER 4

For three whole days, life was wonderful for Laura. She woke early on Saturday morning, thinking about her dragons, and wrote for hours before anyone else stirred. When her parents eventually got up, she had fifty-seven different species and had documented their characteristics and habits in minute detail. There was the huge green sea dragon with burnt-orange wings and long, sharp claws, and the tiny rose-pink morning dragon, which appeared at dawn. There was the scaly old charcoal dragon whose eyes glowed in the dark and whose broad, pulsating nostrils let out great bursts of flame, and the delicate moon dragon, which was visible only in moonlight. She was entranced by them all.

Then at lunchtime, Harry arrived in a flurry of excitement and enthusiasm.

"Good day to you all. And what a wonderful day it is!" he exclaimed, jumping out of the car and throwing his arms wide, as though embracing the whole world. "Love is in the air."

He then embraced a woman, who had jumped out the other side and was standing, laughing, beside the rosebushes. She suddenly burst into an aria.

"This is Isabella. She's an opera singer," Harry explained airily, starting to unload boxes of food. "She hasn't been discovered yet, but she's very good."

Laura smiled at her shyly and took the rope of garlic Harry was handing to her.

"I've come to cook," Harry continued. "I can't sculpt at the moment—I've lost the urge—so I may as well cook. Obviously, that's where my creative energy is channeled right now. I am channeling life."

Harry waved a bunch of parsley under Laura's nose, and she started to giggle. "Can I help you cook?" she asked, taking the parsley.

"You certainly may. We'll start right away. I hope you haven't eaten."

"Of course we haven't." Laura ran over to the door and held it open for Harry and her father to carry in the boxes. She wondered where they were going to store all the provisions.

As soon as Harry saw the table, he swept the newspapers off it onto the floor and began laying out the ingredients for lunch. Laura hastily picked up the papers, then washed her hands and waited for instructions. By the time her parents and Isabella came back into the kitchen after a tour of the house, Laura was rolling out pastry and Harry was dicing onions. His hands flew across the chopping board.

"Look. The table has become a still life," declared Laura's mother, pulling up a chair. "I'm going to draw those vegetables." She reached for a pencil and paper and started sketching.

"What are you cooking?" called Laura's father from the pantry. He was searching for a new bag of coffee beans.

"A vegetable tart. And tonight I will cook my Saturday specialty." Harry brandished his knife in the air. "It only tastes good on Saturdays. It's a ragout from an old Hungarian recipe."

"We should set up a table in the empty room beside the studio," suggested Isabella, waving her dark red fingernails in an expansive gesture toward the hall, setting her bangles jangling. "It can be the dining room. You have all this glorious space here and you're hardly using it. We should fill it. We should fill it with life!" She burst into song again, something high and trilling about spring and rebirth.

Laura's father laughed. "We'll leave that to you and Laura."

"And we'll make it wonderful, won't we, Laura?" said Isabella, her eyes alight. "Harry, you can cook a special feast on Sunday. We'll have the room ready by then." She beckoned to Laura. "Let's see what we can find."

Laura looked questioningly at Harry, and he nodded. "The pastry is finished. Off you go."

She leaped up. "I know where there are some curtains."

"Show me." Isabella took Laura's hand and danced her out of the kitchen.

As Laura led the way down the hall to the small room they used for storage, her heart soared. It was lovely to feel that they were not alone in the world, to be surrounded once again by like-minded people.

When Isabella saw the curtains, she was captivated. "These are velvet," she said. "Real old velvet. Look at the color and the texture. Wherever did you find them?"

"They were in the attic." Laura glowed with pride at her discovery. "I found them in a box."

"Was there anything else in the attic that we could use?"

"Come and see." Laura raced Isabella up the wide staircase and across the landing to the narrow stairs that led to the attic. They had to bend to go through the low door. A little light was filtering in through the cobwebs over the skylight, but the corners were dark and full of mystery. The whole space smelled of dust and dry timber, and the floor creaked as they walked across it.

"Look at this," cried Isabella, pulling out a chair with an elaborately carved back and a broken seat. "And there's another one over there. We should be able to fix them. They'll look grand in the dining room."

Laura nodded, full of excitement. "This is where I found the curtains," she said, lifting the lid off a large packing case. They both leaned over to look in, bumped heads, and came up laughing.

The box was empty except for some assorted cutlery, all rather old and battered, and a heavy candlestick.

"This will be perfect on the table," said Isabella, carrying the candlestick over to the skylight to examine it more closely. "I think it's silver. We can polish it up, and it'll look wonderful. Let's take everything we've found downstairs."

As she was passing the chairs through the door to Isabella, Laura noticed a piece of cardboard on the floor near one of the boxes. Quietly, she slipped it into her pocket before joining Isabella on the landing. Then they struggled down the stairs. The chairs were surprisingly heavy, and they were both glad to reach the new dining room and deposit them by the window.

"We'll need a table," said Isabella, surveying the space. "And some more chairs and candles." She picked up the candlestick, squinting at it. "We'll go on an expedition tomorrow. It will be great. We'll take Harry's car and go shopping."

Laura hesitated. "We can't spend much money," she said.

"Don't worry." Isabella threw her arm around Laura's shoulder. "I'm an expert at shopping on a shoestring."

It was not until later, when Laura was snuggled up in her room with Samson, writing, that she dug her hand into her pocket and felt something unexpected. It was the piece of cardboard she had picked up in the attic—a tattered postcard with a picture of a wide boulevard beside the sea. There were palms lining the street and people in old-fashioned clothes strolling along it. The writing on the back was foreign. Perhaps

French, she thought. Laura leaned the picture up against some books beside her bed, and that night she fell asleep telling herself stories about it.

The next morning, Isabella and Laura set off for the local secondhand shop in Harry's car, a battered 1967 Citroën, which Laura's mother described as a shark. Laura liked to drive in it because it rose on a cushion of air whenever the motor started. But Isabella was not very good at maneuvering such a large vehicle, so they had to park some distance from the shops. As they walked down the main street, Laura tried to look inconspicuous beside Isabella, who was wearing a scarlet hat, a long black coat, and extraordinarily large and noisy earrings.

Fortunately, she only saw one person from school: Leon Murphy. He was walking on the other side of the street with a tall man who stooped and whose hair fell untidily over his face. Laura wondered if this might be Leon's father—though he didn't look like a criminal, just an old man. Then he smiled, and she realized he was much younger than she had first thought. It was just the way he was walking that made him look old. At that moment Leon glanced in her direction. She felt her face redden and turned back to Isabella.

The secondhand shop was overflowing with used furniture and bric-a-brac. Laura expected Isabella to knock something over with her sweeping coat and flamboyant gestures, but she managed to move quite easily through the crowded rooms. Soon, they had found a table and lots of candles and a variety of plates. Then, armed with these treasures, they returned home to transform the room.

They hung the swaths of velvet on one wall. "It is like a medieval tapestry," said Isabella, although Laura wondered how it could be a tapestry if it had no picture on it. They placed candles on boxes under the windowsills, and Isabella swirled a sheet over the table. In the middle, she arranged an elaborate pile of vegetables and fruit, entwined with ivy. They cut more trails of ivy and twisted them around the candles. Then Laura found some empty wine bottles, and they filled these with branches from one of the plum trees.

"We must dress up," said Isabella, catching hold of Laura and spinning her around. "We must look as though we belong in the room. But we won't tell anyone. It will be a surprise."

At dinnertime, they made a spectacular entrance dressed in long skirts, with gleaming earrings dangling from their ears and Isabella's theatrical makeup outlining their eyes. The candles were lit, and Isabella was singing. Laura looked at the table, laden with Harry's delicious food and Isabella's wonderful centerpiece, at the wineglasses sparkling in the candlelight, and at the faces of her parents and Harry, laughing in surprise. She imagined they had been transported to a faraway palace. They were no longer surrounded by the town. School was a million miles away. Outside the walls a wonderful, pine-scented forest had sprung up, and in the night sky her dragons were circling, wild and free. Their fiery breath sent showers of red falling through the darkness. It was an enchanted place. She wished she could stay there forever.

## CHAPTER 5

After the excitement of the banquet and the long, lazy day that followed it, Tuesday morning arrived with awful finality. Laura stumbled into the kitchen, grumpy and miserable. Even when Samson, trying to catch a moth, leaped into the air and landed in a pile of baskets, she couldn't raise a smile.

"Why the long face?" asked Isabella, who was the only other person up.

"I hate school." Laura collapsed onto the nearest chair and reached for the milk carton.

"Why?"

"Everyone stares at me."

"That's good," exclaimed Isabella. "I love it when people stare at me." Her bracelets jangled as she swept her dark curls back from her face and rolled her eyes at Laura.

"Please, Isabella, don't start to sing," begged Laura. "I'm not feeling very strong."

"But music makes you strong," Isabella cried, and burst into an aria anyway.

Laura gulped down her milk and escaped into her parents' room. She sat on the edge of their four-poster bed, looking at the traces of murals on the walls, wishing she could disappear into them.

"I don't want to go to school," she began.

"You always say that." Her mother smiled.

"But today I *really* don't want to go to school. Can't I stay home? I promise I'll go tomorrow."

"It won't be any better tomorrow," her father said, propping his head on his elbow to look across at her.

"Then I could stay home tomorrow too, and the day after that. And the day after that. *Why* do I have to go to school?"

"You know why you have to go to school," replied her mother. "The reasons don't change, just like your questions don't change."

"But today is going to be really bad. Really, really bad. I can feel it."

"It will certainly be bad if you're late," said her father. "Now, off you go. You're spoiling my beauty sleep. I was working until four o'clock to get my article finished."

*Nobody understands*, thought Laura, sliding off the bed.

"The day will be over before you know it," said her mother, kissing her.

"No, it won't. It will go on forever. It will be bad forever."

Laura walked as slowly as she could and arrived at school just before the bell. She glared at the students milling around the locker room. Why couldn't there be people like Isabella and Harry at school? When they were young, of course. Or like her parents. Or like her. Why did she have to be so different? She pulled her books irritably from her bag, and her lunch fell out. Her apple rolled across the floor, bruising.

Kylie, Maddy, and Janie were ahead of her as she crossed the courtyard toward the art room. She ran to catch up with them.

"Did you do anything over the long weekend?" asked Maddy.

Laura gave her usual evasive reply: "Nothing much." Then she added, "We had some friends visit." That seemed safe enough. "What about you, Maddy?"

"We went down to Lorne. It was awesome. We spent all day at the beach. There was even some sun. Look at my tan." Maddy lifted her skirt to show off her legs.

"You're so lucky," grumbled Kylie. "I wish we'd gone away. We never go anywhere. It's so not fair."

"I think I saw your friends." Janie turned to Laura. "They were shopping on the main street. Do they wear strange clothes?"

*Here we go again*, thought Laura. "Sometimes."

"They looked really weird. Are they weird?"

"No!" Laura dug her fingernails into her palms. "They're just—they're just a bit different."

"You can say that again!" Janie grinned at the others. "Spooky, I'd say. Really *spooky*." Kylie and Maddy giggled and nudged Laura.

Laura tried to smile, but the thought of Harry and Isabella being laughed at made her feel horrible. She just knew today was going to be bad. She sighed and headed into class.

Finally, she reached the last class of the day, English. This should have been one of her favorite subjects but Miss Grisham's classes were so dry and repetitive that Laura always had trouble concentrating in them.

She fit her chin into her hands and lifted her gaze to that patch of blue through the window that was her escape. Her thoughts wandered to her dragon book. She would be home soon and able to work on it. She conjured up a number of her favorite species and reviewed their habitats and characteristics.

Suddenly, an idea for a new dragon flew into her mind. She saw the dragon clearly in that blue sky, its wings a translucent silver, its eyes full of reflections. A terrible, urgent need to capture the image before it flew away seized her. Hardly daring to breathe, she reached into her desk and drew out a piece of paper. Then, shielded by Jamie Robertson's back, Laura started sketching.

She was almost finished when she realized that Miss Grisham's eyes were fixed on her. She dropped her pen and covered the image with her arm—but too late.

"You feel no need to join us in this exercise, Laura Horton?" inquired Miss Grisham.

"No, Miss Grisham . . . I mean, yes. I was just writing something down."

"What?"

Laura went cold. "Nothing. Nothing important."

"Let me see."

"It's nothing, Miss Grisham. Please, I'll put it away."

"Bring it here."

Laura looked down at the paper she was shielding. The tiny dragon's face peeped out from under her arm. She couldn't give it to Miss Grisham. She just couldn't. This was her own private world; it would be like laying her soul bare.

She gulped. "No."

Everyone gasped, even Miss Grisham.

"Laura, this is the last time I will ask you. *Bring* the paper here."

A blackness descended over Laura. She could not see the classroom, the desks, or the students. She could only see Miss Grisham. Her heart was throbbing so powerfully, it felt as though it had taken over her whole body. There was nothing but the *thump, thump, thump* of its beat. Laura picked up the paper and deliberately, desperately, tore the tiny dragon in half. She continued to tear it over and over again until the pieces lay scattered like blossoms over her desk.

"Outside, Laura," ordered Miss Grisham in the iciest voice Laura had ever heard.

Laura swept the pieces into her hand and clenched them in her fist. Then she walked to the door, darkness surrounding her. She felt as though she was walking through a tunnel, but the tunnel had eyes that gazed at her with fascination, horror, fear.

She stared straight ahead. Only as she reached the door did she glance sideways and glimpse Leon watching her with a mixture of surprise and amusement. She wrenched the door open and stepped outside.

The hallway was long and cold. Empty. Laura stood hesitating, wondering what she should do; she had never been in this position before.

Her eyes fixed on a poster flapping in the breeze. READ MORE BOOKS, it said. COME TO THE LIBRARY. If only she could. She would be able to hide there among the books. But that was not possible now: Miss Grisham had opened the door and was stepping outside. Laura looked down at her feet. At least Miss Grisham would never see *her* book, but a little part of it was lost forever, and Laura felt anger rising within her. She lifted her eyes and faced Miss Grisham.

"Now perhaps you can tell me what that was all about, Laura," her teacher said.

"I am sorry, but I don't think so," replied Laura.

Miss Grisham gasped again. "Really, Laura, I don't know what has gotten into you. You have always been such a good student."

Laura clenched her hand more tightly around the

fragments of paper and said nothing. Miss Grisham stared at her. She stared at her for so long, Laura thought they were going to be standing there until the bell rang.

"I don't know what to do with you," said Miss Grisham eventually. "You have the potential to do really well, Laura, but you never put in quite enough effort. And now this." Laura's eyes slid back to the poster. "Is there something troubling you? Something wrong at home?"

"No!" Laura spoke too vehemently and saw that her teacher did not believe her. *Just like Miss Grisham to misinterpret everything,* she thought. Miss Grisham was looking at her with pity and concern now instead of anger. Laura wondered what appalling things she was imagining.

"Well, I'm going to let you off this time, Laura, but if something like this happens again, I shall have to speak to Mr. Jameson."

"Yes, Miss Grisham."

"Now come back inside."

"Yes, Miss Grisham."

Laura followed her into the classroom and sat down, aware of the battery of eyes still on her. Would she ever live this down? This was the sort of thing people remembered forever. She would always be the girl who tore up a piece of paper in front of Miss Grisham. She felt a lump in her throat. Could things get any worse?

As soon as the class was over, Laura bolted for the gate, abandoning all thoughts of picking up her bag. Any homework would just have to wait. If she went to the locker room, she would face a barrage of questions. She set off at a fast pace but was only halfway down the hill when Leon appeared beside her.

"So what was on the paper?" he asked, a hint of laughter in his voice.

"Something."

Leon watched her for a moment, then said, "You and I are alike, you know."

"We are not!" Laura flashed, turning an outraged face toward him.

"We both have secrets."

"Everyone has secrets." She started to walk faster.

"Not like ours."

Laura shot him a furious look. "I don't have secrets. I just didn't want everyone to see. I didn't want Miss Grisham to see."

"We have secrets because we're forced to."

"I don't know what you are talking about." Laura tossed her head. "I don't have secrets. Not the sort you mean. And I don't want to talk about it. Go away."

Leon continued to walk beside her, his step in time with hers. "You live in that house on the hill, don't you?" he asked after a while.

Laura glared at him. "There are lots of houses on lots of hills."

"Not like yours."

Those words again. *Not like yours.* Laura felt something snap inside her. Everything was always not like hers. Her house was different. Her parents were different. Their friends were different. No one else at school was writing a book about dragons, and no one else would have torn up part of it if they had been. They wouldn't have cared. And now Leon Murphy, who didn't talk to anyone, was talking to her. She must be terribly, terribly different.

Tears welled in her eyes. "Go away," she shouted. "I don't want to talk to you. I don't want to talk to anyone. Just leave me alone."

"OK." Leon thrust his hands into his pockets and strode off. Laura could see him ahead of her, growing smaller, his large shorts flapping as he walked. She watched him until he turned in to Mrs. Murphy's garden and disappeared around the side of the house.

How dare he suggest that they were alike, she seethed, quickening her pace now that he had gone. How dare he say that she had secrets like his! Then she stopped abruptly, struck by what he had actually said.

Just what *were* Leon Murphy's secrets?

Samson emerged from the bushes as she came through the gates. She scooped him up, hugging him fiercely. He leaped out of her arms in protest and ran toward the kitchen, Laura close behind.

It felt strange arriving home with no bag weighing her down. She wondered if anyone would notice, but no one did. They were all busy with their own projects. Her mother was in the studio working on a sculpture for a neighboring town. Her father had an article to finish. Harry was cooking, and Isabella was chopping vegetables.

"Hello, kiddo," Isabella called out. "How was the big wide world?"

"Bad," said Laura.

Isabella broke into a high-pitched lament.

"Not now, Isabella," grumbled Harry. "I have to concentrate." He turned to Laura. "We are cooking a farewell feast. We have to go."

Now they were leaving, too. *More misery*, she thought, and continued through to the studio. Pushing open the door, she found her mother frowning in concentration over a piece of stone.

"Hello, honey bear," she said without looking up. "How was your day?"

"Bad," replied Laura.

"There's some cake in the cupboard."

"I don't want any cake."

"All right. Can you close the door? I don't want this dust to get everywhere."

Laura closed the door and went to her room. She climbed onto the bed and pulled her knees up under her chin. She didn't want to work on her dragon book anymore; it was tainted now. Every time she looked at it, she would think of Miss Grisham. But she felt terribly lonely without it. She stared out the window at the dark magnolia. What would she do now?

Harry and Isabella's dinner was not a success. Laura's mother was preoccupied, her father was irritable, and Laura was wretched. Even Isabella didn't feel like singing. They chomped their way through *canard à l'orange* followed by salad and chocolate mousse as though they were eating baked beans on toast.

At the end, Harry rose and raised his glass. "Farewell," he said. "We are already all somewhere else, and it is good to go when the time is right. Thank you for your hospitality. Let us drink to friendship."

They all drank, Laura filling her glass with water from the jug on the table. But when she put her glass back down, she felt more miserable than ever. It seemed dreadful to be drinking to something that she did not have. Friends. Real friends, her own age, doing their own thing.

She slipped off her chair and crept away to bed. Lying there, listening to the wind outside and the branch of the magnolia tree tapping against her window, she thought of Leon. It occurred to Laura that perhaps their strange conversation on the way home had been an attempt at friendship on Leon's behalf.

But she didn't want him as a friend. No one was friends with Leon.

She pulled the blankets up over her head and cried herself to sleep.

## ⟡ CHAPTER 6 ⟡

When morning came, Laura refused to get up. When her father quoted more Longfellow at her—"Lives of great men all remind us we can make our lives sublime"—she did not say, as she usually did, "What about the women?" Instead, she burst into tears. And when her mother arrived, pulling on the knitted coat she used as a bathrobe, Laura huddled under the comforter and would not come out.

"What's the matter, honey bear?" asked her mother, trying to hug her through the covers.

"Go away."

"Are you not feeling well?"

Laura dug deeper into the bed, clutching the comforter tightly around her. "No, I feel sick." It was true; her stomach churned every time she thought about having to go back to school.

"Let me feel your forehead."

Laura did not move.

"Why don't you come out and we can talk about it?"

Laura wriggled down until she was just a small hump at the end of the bed. She could hardly breathe.

"Running away won't help." This was her father. "Why don't you tell us what the problem is?"

"I've told you," came the muffled reply. "I hate school."

"But why?"

*Why? Because nobody understands. Because I'm lonely. Because I'm different. Because everything I do leads to trouble.* The answers drummed in her head, but Laura didn't reply.

"I'm going to make some coffee," said her father. "Then we can talk."

Laura heard her parents leave the room and came up for air.

When they returned, her father was carrying Samson. "Here's a bit of furry comfort I found skulking around the kitchen."

Laura gave a watery smile and reached for the cat, burying her face in his fur.

"Now, how are you feeling sick?" asked her mother. "Is it your head or your stomach?"

"It's . . . everything."

Her mother felt the part of her forehead not covered by Samson's fur. "You don't feel hot," she said.

"Let me feel." Her father smiled down at her as he, too, felt her forehead. "Ah, you're right. She doesn't feel hot—she feels miserable. That's my diagnosis. Misery. Am I right?"

"Maybe," muttered Laura.

"So the question is, what are we going to do about it?"

"Should we go up to the school to discuss it with your teachers?" suggested her mother.

Laura sat up immediately, almost dropping Samson in horror. "No!"

"But, honey bear, if there is a problem, we need to sort it out."

"You can't sort out hating school, except by not going," shouted Laura. All the same, she climbed out of bed. The thought of her parents going to the school was too dreadful to contemplate. They would understand about her tearing up the paper, and they would try to explain it to Miss Grisham, but this would not resolve the problem. Her parents could not resolve the problem because *they* were the problem, and she couldn't tell them that. Despite everything, she didn't want them to change; she loved them as they were.

As she headed for the bathroom, she cried tears of frustration. Everything was too complicated—it was the world she wanted to change, and it wouldn't.

It had been strange arriving home without her schoolbag; it was even stranger walking to school without it. All the way she imagined what people would be saying about her, and by the time she reached the gate, her stomach was in knots. Crossing the courtyard was torture. She felt as though everyone was staring at her, as though everyone was talking about her.

She soon found out that she was right; they were. It had not taken long for news about the confrontation with Miss Grisham to begin circulating. Almost everyone in Year Eight had heard some version of it, and rumors were spreading like wildfire. As soon as she entered the locker room, a group of girls pounced on her.

"What was in the note?"

"Was it a love letter?"

Laughter.

"Who was it from?"

"Was it something rude?"

More laughter.

"Come on, tell us. We promise not to tell."

Laura brushed past them and headed for the classroom. Her heart plunging, she saw Kylie and Maddy hovering by the door, waiting for her.

"What was on the paper, Laura?" said Kylie, rushing up. "It must have been really important."

"No, it wasn't. It was nothing." Laura struggled to keep her voice steady.

"You wouldn't have torn it up if it was nothing," said Maddy.

"We'll find out anyway, you know." Kylie pushed her face uncomfortably close to Laura's. "I told you I'd make a good detective. You may as well just tell us."

Fortunately, Mr. Parker arrived at that moment. "Move away," he said, flapping papers at them. "You should be in your seats."

Laura ducked past Kylie and sat down. She hoped the worst was now over. She worked away in class, trying to ignore the whispering around her, and slipped off to the library at recess.

As she was organizing her books after the last class before lunch, however, Kylie, Maddy, and Janie swooped on her again. They were nudging one another and giggling.

"Come on, Laura. Tell us what was on the paper," coaxed Kylie. She twisted the chain around her neck and smiled encouragingly. "We're your friends. We won't tell."

"It was nothing," repeated Laura, stuffing her pens into her pencil case. "I have to go."

"No, you don't. It's lunchtime. You don't have to go anywhere."

Laura looked around. Everyone was packing up to leave. She tried to push past Kylie, but Maddy and Janie blocked her way.

"It must have been a love letter," pressed Kylie. "That's why you won't tell." She raised her voice. "Laura Horton's writing love letters."

The room went quiet as everyone turned toward them.

"Shoosh," Laura hissed. "It wasn't a love letter."

"Laura Horton's writing love letters," chanted Janie and Maddy. "Laura Horton's writing love letters." Maddy snatched Laura's notebook and began flipping through the pages, looking for notes.

"Stop it," cried Laura, making a grab for the notebook and missing. "Stop it."

"Laura Horton's writing love letters," sang out Kylie again, her voice louder than before. Laura felt as though the whole school must be able to hear by now.

"I'm not. I'm not. Stop it. Why won't you stop it?" Laura was pleading, her voice cracking.

Kylie smirked. She leaned forward, her face almost touching Laura's. "Who was it to?"

Laura gulped back tears. Her ears were drumming, and her stomach lurched. All she could think of was getting away. She made another grab for her notebook and it tore as she wrenched it out of Maddy's hand. She gathered up her books in one sweep and started toward the door, but she did not see the bag on the floor. As she fell, her books and pens scattered everywhere. There was a burst of laughter before a voice from the other side of the room said, "Leave her alone." She scrambled to pick up her things, surprised that anyone would stand up for her.

It wasn't until she had reached the door that she realized it was Leon Murphy.

Once she was out of the classroom, Laura began to run. She ran past the hall, across the courtyard, up the stairs, and along the corridor. She did not stop running until she reached the library, the only place she could think of where she would be safe.

To her disappointment, she discovered it was closed, but there was a bench outside, so she sat down, huddled up, and waited. Why hadn't she just shown

Miss Grisham the drawing? Why had it seemed so important? It was all so much worse now, and there was no way back, no way out. She stared at the window and bit her lip to stop the tears from starting again.

"Whatever is the matter?" asked Ms. McAlister, arriving five minutes later, key in hand to open the library, and finding her there.

Laura jumped up and attempted to look as though everything was fine. "Nothing, Ms. McAlister. I wasn't hungry, so I came up early. I wanted to borrow some books."

Eyes still questioning, Ms. McAlister unlocked the door. Laura managed a smile and slipped past her into the safety of the bookshelves. There she leaned her head against the metal shelving and tried to collect her thoughts.

How quickly she had fallen into this nightmare. She had never been popular, but she had never been unpopular, either. Despite her house, despite her parents, she had always managed to cling on and keep her head down. But now, it was all spinning out of control. When had this begun? And why?

Perversely, she thought of Leon. It had all started after he arrived. Not that she thought it was anything he had done; it was just his being there. She frowned.

Somehow she was ending up on the outside and ending up with him.

"Are you sure you're all right?" Ms. McAlister appeared behind her, making her jump.

Laura forced a smile and nodded. Even if she wanted to, how could she explain everything that had happened? How could she explain Leon?

She made a desperate effort to pull herself together. "I'm fine, just a bit tired. We've had some friends staying with us, some late nights." That sounded normal. She didn't have to explain that the friends were Harry and Isabella, nor that the late nights were spent having dinner in a room decorated with ivy and velvet. Laura changed the subject. "I have a project on medieval feasts. I need to find some information on the food they would have eaten."

"You're in the wrong spot," observed Ms. McAlister. "This is the geography section."

Laura knew the librarian didn't believe her, but fortunately a skirmish near the entrance of the library drew Ms. McAlister away to investigate. Seizing the momentary reprieve, Laura hurried to the history section. There she found a pile of books and carried them to a table. Her mind went back to her mantra. *If only I didn't have to go to school. If only I could just stay home*. She pictured her little corner in her big room, the comfort of her blankets and cushions, the pleasure of her things, her dragon book with its delicate drawings and careful anatomical descriptions . . .

She stopped, her thoughts seared with pain. She could never finish her dragon book now. Miss Grisham and Kylie had destroyed it for her. Destroyed it forever.

She tried to focus on an illustration of a medieval feast. Graceful ladies in flowing robes with coned hats and pointed shoes were seated at a long table, conversing with slender young men in doublets and hose. They looked happy, in a delicate sort of way. On the table was a large platter with a huge bird on it. Medieval people ate all sorts of birds, she read. Swans, peacocks, pheasants, and guinea fowl. Large birds were often stuffed with parts of smaller birds. A quail inside a duck inside a chicken inside a swan. Laura frowned, wondering what Harry would make of that, but the thought of Harry made her want to cry again, so she read on. There were no potatoes in England in the fourteenth century, the book said, and very little salt, which would mean never having fries. Warm, greasy, salty, sweet-smelling fries. She then remembered that she hadn't had lunch and there was the whole afternoon to get through on an empty stomach. Laura stared at the revelers in their embroidered clothes, enjoying their laden table and aching to transport herself there. Or anywhere, so long as it was far, far away from school.

She closed the book with a bang. How would she ever survive the afternoon?

## ❖ CHAPTER 7 ❖

By the time the bell finally rang at the end of the day, Laura was feeling utterly crushed. She trailed down the road, munching through the duck sandwiches that Harry had packed for her lunch. She barely tasted them, wondering how on earth she was going to endure four and a quarter more years of school before she would be free. She was almost at the train crossing before she realized that she was not alone; Leon was walking beside her.

"How long have you been there?" she snapped.

"Been where?"

"There. Here. Following me."

"I wasn't following you."

Laura eyed him disbelievingly. "I can look after myself, you know. I don't need you trailing around."

"Oh, yeah? Like you were looking after yourself at lunchtime?"

Laura swallowed the last of her sandwich and

folded the wrapper into a little square. "That was different."

Leon raised an eyebrow.

They crossed the train tracks, and he turned toward his grandmother's house. Mrs. Murphy was in the garden, digging. She looked up at the sound of their voices, brushing back her gray hair with a dirty hand, which left smudges of soil mixed with sweat on her forehead.

"Hello, Grandma," said Leon.

Mrs. Murphy straightened up. "Are you going to introduce me to your friend?"

Laura was horrified. *I am* not *his friend*, she thought, looking across at Leon. He too appeared to be weighing how to reply.

"This is a girl from school, Laura Horton."

"Hello, Mrs. Murphy." Laura smiled awkwardly and turned to go.

"You live in the Visconti house, don't you?" said Mrs. Murphy, wiping her hands on the side of her skirt and coming over to the fence.

Laura turned back in surprise. "The Visconti house?"

"The big house up on the hill."

"Yes," said Laura.

"I remember when Mr. Visconti still lived there. He was very old then, and I was just a little girl, a tiny slip of a thing. You wouldn't think it to see me now, would you?"

Laura did not know what to say, so she said nothing.

"Who was Mr. Visconti, Grandma?" asked Leon, sliding his bag off his shoulder.

"He was an Italian gentleman. Some people said that he had been an ambassador or a consul and that he had traveled all over the world. Others said he was a professor. No one really knew. He lived in the big house on his own."

Mrs. Murphy paused, gazing toward the road. Laura sensed that she was seeing something neither Laura nor Leon could see.

"Every morning he would go for a walk," continued Mrs. Murphy. "He wore a suit with a waistcoat and a watch chain, and there was always a flower in his buttonhole. He had long white hair and was very frail. He used a walking stick—an elegant one, black, I think, with a silver knob. We children used to laugh at him, I'm ashamed to say. He was such a strange figure with his flowers and his hat—he wore a straw hat in summer, I remember. No one wore hats like that. He was so straight and so old. We would run after him sometimes, whispering, but he never seemed to mind. I don't think he even noticed us."

"Didn't he have any family?" asked Laura, drawn into the conversation despite herself.

"Not that I know of. Strange, isn't it? Him settling here in this small town with his grand house. All alone. People said there were paintings on the walls of his house. Murals."

"There were." Laura nodded. "Some of them are still there."

"Fancy that! I didn't really believe it." Mrs. Murphy pushed back her hair again and sighed. "You never know with stories."

"What are the murals like?" asked Leon.

"There aren't many left now. Just patches. They were scenes, I think. Gardens and columns."

"The outside inside," said Leon, grinning.

Laura smiled a little smile, too. She liked that idea, the outside inside. "Sometimes the outside is literally inside now," she volunteered. "The rain comes in through parts of the roof. And there is ivy growing under the door."

"Gardens tend to do that if you let them," agreed Mrs. Murphy. "They creep into everything."

Laura looked at Mrs. Murphy's garden. It had not been allowed to creep; rows of carrots, lettuce, and tomatoes were growing in straight lines. Two rosebushes had been pruned back to a few bare stalks, and a lemon tree was similarly stark. Still, there were green shoots pushing up through the dark earth and grass growing over the borders. Perhaps a little creeping was going on, after all.

"Would you like some tomatoes to take home?" asked Mrs. Murphy.

Laura wasn't sure that she would, but she didn't want to hurt Mrs. Murphy's feelings, so she said, "Yes, if you have enough."

"Sure. We have more than we can eat. Leon, go and fetch a plastic bag for me from the kitchen." Mrs. Murphy bent over, groaning a little, and started to gather the ripe fruit. "These are the very last of the season," she said, "but they should still have some flavor. Don't they smell good?" She held up one for Laura to smell.

Laura sniffed and was surprised by the distinctive tang of the freshly picked fruit. She tried to think of a word to describe it but couldn't.

When Leon returned, Mrs. Murphy put the tomatoes in the bag and handed it to Laura.

"It's been nice meeting you, Laura Horton," she

said. "Stop and have a chat next time you're passing."

As Laura climbed the hill to her house, swinging the rather grubby plastic bag, she realized with astonishment that she was feeling better. Thoughts of the terrible day had been replaced by thoughts of the mysterious Mr. Visconti who used to live in her house. All sorts of questions about him were buzzing in her head. Why had he come to the town? Why had he built the house? What sort of person had he been? She wondered why she had never thought about the house like that before. After some fruitcake and juice, she began wandering around, looking for traces of Mr. Visconti. She imagined him leaning on his walking cane, moving slowly from room to room, with all his things around him.

In her mind, she filled the rooms with paintings in heavy gilt frames, tapestries, and silver candlesticks. She hung curtains over the drafty windows and placed mementos of his travels on the mantelpieces and tables—cloisonné vases, Chinese fans, scenes of the pyramids—all in exquisite taste, like Mr. Visconti. All old, like Mr. Visconti. She could almost see him in the shadows, almost smell the musty, perfumed air, almost hear the sound of labored breathing, of clocks ticking, of a gramophone playing.

In her parents' bedroom, she stood for a long time, staring at the fragments of paint, wondering what Mr. Visconti did in this room where the outside was inside. Did he sit here, remembering Italy, the Italy of his childhood? Or was it a fantasy world for him, a garden of delight? An escape? Then she came back to the questions she had been asking herself on the way home. Why was he here at all, in this small Australian town? And why was he alone? The questions jumbled and jostled in her mind.

There were no answers, however, and she was getting hungry. She remembered the tomatoes and wished that Harry was still there to cook them. Then, because he wasn't, she decided she would try cooking them herself and headed back to the kitchen to leaf through the pages of her mother's old cookbook. When she found an Italian recipe for tomato sauce, she stopped. The recipe looked relatively simple, and the sauce could be eaten with spaghetti, which she knew they had. She smiled. It would be right to eat it in Mr. Visconti's house.

Luckily, most of the ingredients were in the cupboard, although she did have to improvise a little. Harry had left cloves of garlic hanging by the door, so she crushed them and added them to the onions.

Their smell made her think of faraway places and exotic tastes.

When the sauce was ready, she put the spaghetti into a pot of boiling water and set the table. It was still early, but she thought that it would be good to eat before they were all ravenous, which didn't happen very often.

The kitchen table looked bare with only three places set, so she decided to pick some of the red roses from the bush outside the ballroom window to put in the center. As she stood on tiptoe to reach a particularly high bud, she wondered if Mr. Visconti had planted the bush. The bud was perfect, its petals still tightly folded, full of promise. Did Mr. Visconti put a bud like this in his buttonhole? Did he stop here, where she was standing, and smell this perfume in the evening air? And if he did, did it make him sad because he was alone, a long way from his birthplace? Or glad because he was here in a strange new land, smelling old smells in a new world?

Her mother exclaimed with delight when she saw the table, and her father sniffed at his bowl of spaghetti appreciatively.

"Mmm, this smells delectable," he said. "I wonder what it tastes like."

Laura watched as he put a large forkful in his mouth and chewed it solemnly, gazing up at the ceiling.

"Perfect." He grinned at her. "I hope there's enough for seconds."

Laura saw her parents exchange glances, and she knew that they were both relieved to see that she was no longer wallowing in her misery.

"These tomatoes taste quite different from the ones in the shops," said Laura's mother, wiping her bowl with a chunk of bread. "Mrs. Murphy must be a very good gardener."

"She's a very tidy one," replied Laura. She paused, then added, "She said she knew the man who built this house. Well, remembered seeing him, anyway."

"He must have been very old then," remarked Laura's father. "The house dates to 1895."

"He was. And Mrs. Murphy was very young. She said he used to go for a walk every morning."

"His name was Visconti, wasn't it?" said Laura's mother.

Laura's eyes widened. "How did you know that?"

"From the papers that came with the deed of the property. I believe there are records and photographs down in the Heritage Society rooms at the library."

Laura felt a tremor of excitement. An idea had come to her. A wonderful idea. She would find out all about Mr. Visconti. She would find out who he was and what he was doing here. She would get to know him. Now that she had lost her dragon world, this would be a new one to explore, another secret place.

## CHAPTER 8

Laura did not complain about going to school the next morning. She got up early and set off with time to spare. As she came down the hill and looked out over the town, she tried to imagine what it must have been like when Mr. Visconti arrived and began building his house — her house. How different it must have been from the way it was now. And how different it must have been from Italy.

Her parents had books with pictures of Italy. There were lots of photos of sculptures and paintings, but there were also photos of cobbled streets and stone houses and dark green pines. The skies in the photos were a soft blue, not like the deep bright blue of the Australian skies. Her father's friend Richard had lived in Tuscany, and he was always talking about how different the light was there. She wondered if Mr. Visconti had missed the light of Italy.

The sight of Kylie and Maddy ahead of her

punctured Laura's reflective mood and brought her thoughts crashing down. She managed to avoid the girls, however, and hurried to class. As she was finding a seat, one of the boys crumpled a piece of paper and tossed it at her. "Any more love notes you want to get rid of?" he called out. Laura shot him a wrathful look before burying her nose in her book. She was uncomfortably aware that across the room, Leon was reading, too.

It was French class, and she had plenty of time, after she had finished the exercises, to think about researching Mr. Visconti. She decided that she would start by going to the Heritage Society rooms that afternoon. Maybe there would be old photos of the house in the archives. Maybe there would even be a photo of Mr. Visconti.

She looked at the clock. Only five and a half hours to go. And after math, there were only four and a half hours. If she could just keep focused on this, she might make it through the day. She glanced at Kylie and Maddy, whispering together on the other side of the room. Would she be able to avoid them for five and a half hours?

Somehow she did. When the last bell finally rang, Laura dashed to the locker room and left before Kylie,

Maddy, and Janie arrived. She ran out the gate and headed straight toward town and the public library.

The wide main street with its shady verandas and newly planted trees was busy for a midweek afternoon. Laura walked quickly past a group of kids hanging around Sam's Hamburger Joint and two Year Eight girls coming out of the supermarket with their mothers. She did not slow down until she reached the elaborate cast-iron gates, opening into the parched public gardens.

In front of her was the empty fountain, dominated by a stone sculpture of Neptune, and to her left, guarded by two tall palms, was the library. It was half-old, half-new. The new section was filled with light and was familiar to Laura. She often came there to borrow books. She had never been into the old section, though, a gray Victorian building with a rather forbidding facade and steps that looked as though they were never used. She guessed that this was where the Heritage Society rooms would be. She waited near the information desk in the new section until Mrs. Carlton, the librarian, was free, and then asked how she could find information about Mr. Visconti.

"I'm not sure what we have," replied Mrs. Carlton, "but let's go and look."

Laura followed her through a door and down a gray corridor to a room at the end. It was dark, and the air smelled stale. Heavy curtains were drawn across the window, and the ceiling soared above them. In the dim light Laura could see shelves filled with books and papers. There were more papers on a large table in the center of the room and on a desk under the window. She wondered where Mrs. Carlton would start looking, and Mrs. Carlton, who had just switched on the light, looked as though she was wondering the same thing.

"I think there are papers under *Visconti*," she said, pulling down a box. "Sorry, this is not really my area."

Laura was used to things being easy to find in libraries. She watched, amazed at the confusion, as Mrs. Carlton rifled through various boxes and files until she found a manila folder with some newspaper clippings in it and two slim histories of the town.

"There may be something in these," she suggested. "Bring them out to the front and see what you can find. If you want more information, it would be best to contact a woman named Miss McInnes. She has some connection to the family, I believe. She can be rather difficult, though." Mrs. Carlton smiled at Laura. "You'll need to tread carefully."

Laura gathered up the folder and booklets and followed Mrs. Carlton out to the light-filled extension. "Maybe I'll find what I'm looking for in these papers," she said, "and then I won't have to bother Miss McInnes."

Mrs. Carlton headed back to her desk, and Laura found a free cubicle, where she sat down. Holding her breath in anticipation, she opened the folder. The newspaper clippings were yellow and brittle with age. Laura gently turned them over, looking first for a photograph of Mr. Visconti.

When she found one, however, she was a little disappointed. He appeared so old and frail, leaning on his stick in his neat three-piece suit and, except for his long hair, somehow seemed very conventional. She turned to another, larger photograph and sat looking at it, trying to imagine this man in her house, sitting in her rooms and strolling through her garden. She frowned. It was hard to do.

There was also a photograph of the house not long after it had been built. The garden was almost bare, except for a few bushes, the monkey puzzle tree, and the palm. It gave her a strange feeling to see it looking so familiar and yet so different. There were no sheds at the side, but there was a sort of fernery, which had obviously since been pulled down.

The only other photograph in the folder was one of the house taken before it was auctioned the first time. The garden was much more developed then, and Laura could see quite clearly the rosebushes under the ballroom window. She turned back to the photograph of Mr. Visconti and, yes, there was a dark shadow on his lapel where a flower must have been placed in his buttonhole.

After she had examined the photographs, Laura started reading the articles and the histories. She was so engrossed in them that she jumped when Mrs. Carlton came up behind her with another picture of the house. It was in a book about architecture. In this photograph there was a statue of a young woman in the garden. Her hair was blowing in the breeze, and she was holding a book. *Strange*, thought Laura, gazing at it intently. *This is certainly not in the garden anymore. What could have happened to it?* She read the caption beneath the photograph, but there was no mention of Mr. Visconti or the statue.

Mrs. Carlton was still hovering beside her. She smiled at Laura. "The library will be closing soon. Were the files useful?"

Laura nodded. "Yes," she replied, a little dazed.

"But I won't be able to remember it all. Can I photocopy the articles?"

"Of course. Just be careful you don't crease them."

It took all Laura's spare change to photocopy everything. Mrs. Carlton was preparing to lock the front door as Laura dropped her last coin into the machine and watched the last sheet of paper appear on the other side. Then she started the long walk home, thinking about her discoveries.

Some of the information had been very confusing. One article had said that Mr. Visconti was born in Milan, and another that he came from Turin. One said that he had been a diplomat, but in the booklet it said that he had been a "man of leisure," whatever that meant. There was even debate about when he died, which seemed very odd to Laura. Weren't there proper records? she wondered.

What appeared certain was that he was wealthy, that he was musical, and that he lived alone, completely alone. In her imagination she saw an old man who had tried to build a small piece of paradise in a dusty, sun-bleached town. A man who had planted palms and roses in the garden and painted arbors on the walls of his house.

But why he was there and what he did in that big house remained a complete mystery. She realized that if she was going to find an answer, she would have to brave Miss McInnes. She was just trying to figure out how when Leon Murphy came up behind her.

"What were you doing at the library?" he asked.

Laura started. "What do you mean?" She eyed him warily. "How did you know I was there?"

Leon shrugged. "I was just returning some books. I saw you."

Laura bit her lip. "Well, it's none of your business." She expected him to storm off, but he didn't. He fell into step beside her and took some chewing gum from his pocket and offered her a piece. Laura shook her head and fixed her eyes on the road ahead. Why was he talking to her? Couldn't he see that she didn't want to talk to him? She hoped desperately that no one would see them together.

They were almost at the train tracks before she spoke. "The tomatoes were delicious. Would you please tell your grandmother?"

"Sure. She's pretty good at growing vegetables."

"Yes." They crossed the tracks and reached Mrs. Murphy's house.

"How did you get to be so good at math?" asked Laura, suddenly.

"Genes, I guess. My dad's pretty good at math."

"Where does he live, your dad?" But as soon as she asked the question, Laura knew that she shouldn't have. Leon's face closed over.

"I've got to go," he said. "See you around." Swinging open the gate, he disappeared around the side of the house.

Laura stared after him, fuming. *What makes him think he can say whatever he likes and then refuse to answer questions himself? And what is it about his dad that is so mysterious?* She kicked a stone crossly, thinking about all the rumors. Surely Kylie was just making things up. But Leon had looked so lost when she mentioned his father. Perhaps it was true. Laura felt a stab of remorse. She should have guessed that he wouldn't want to talk about him.

Well, what did it matter, anyway? she told herself, hurrying on. He was just Leon Murphy from the white house by the train tracks. She pushed the thought of him away and brought up the image of Mr. Visconti: elegant, exotic, strolling down the hill with his fine black cane and a rose in his buttonhole. He bowed to her slightly, inclining his head.

## CHAPTER 9

It was not until Friday afternoon that Laura summoned up enough courage to visit Miss McInnes. Her house was on the other side of the town, near the gas station. It was a small weatherboard cottage with a neat, well-kept garden and white painted stones lining the path from the wire gate to the wire security screen. As Laura walked along the path, she expected someone to pop out and tell her she was trespassing.

She reached the front door and rang the bell, listening to the buzz deep in the heart of the house, a shrill, annoying sound like an egg timer. It seemed to Laura it would be very uncomfortable to have a doorbell that sounded as though something had just boiled.

Miss McInnes took a long time coming to the door, and when she did, she left the wire screen closed, speaking through it. Her tone was uninviting. "Yes?"

Laura took a deep breath and launched into her rehearsed speech. "My name is Laura Horton. I live in the Visconti house and I am trying to find out something about its history. Mrs. Carlton at the library thought you might be able to help me."

"What do you want to know?"

It was hard talking through a wire screen. Laura wondered if she might ask Miss McInnes to open it but decided that it would be no use — Miss McInnes was looking at her very distrustfully. It occurred to Laura that she must be a similar age to Mrs. Murphy, but Mrs. Murphy was large and comfortable and didn't worry about her clothes at all, whereas Miss McInnes was small and thin and probably worried a great deal about what she wore. Laura suddenly wished that she'd had time to change before coming.

"Do you know why Mr. Visconti settled here?"

"No one knows that," replied Miss McInnes sharply. But the shadow of something, a memory or perhaps a scrap of gossip, crossed her face, and Laura was sure she knew more than she was saying.

She tried again. "Someone must have an idea, a suggestion."

"Not that I've heard." Miss McInnes paused. "Have you read the local history pamphlet?"

"Yes."

"Well, I can't tell you much more. Mr. Visconti came here from Milan, I believe. He built the house and he lived there. On his own. He kept to himself. No one knew him well. I'm sorry; I can't really help you with your project."

"It's not a project, Miss McInnes." Laura tried to look as enthusiastic and trustworthy as possible. "I'm just interested because I live there."

Miss McInnes was not impressed. "Well, that's all I know. Now you'll have to go, I'm afraid. I've got chutney simmering on the stove, and I have to get back to it."

There was nothing for Laura to do but say thank you and leave.

As she walked away, thoughts were spinning in her head. She felt sure that Miss McInnes was hiding something, but she also knew from her own experience that making someone talk if they didn't want to was not easy. It seemed strange, though, that Miss McInnes should be so secretive. Why would she not want to talk about Mr. Visconti?

Still puzzling about Miss McInnes, Laura came over the hill and looked down to the train tracks and Mrs. Murphy's house. Mrs. Murphy was, as usual, working in her garden, and Laura watched her thoughtfully. Mrs. Murphy and Miss McInnes had both lived in the town for a very long time, possibly all their lives, and they were about the same age. Despite their differences, they must know each other. Maybe Mrs. Murphy would help her find out what Miss McInnes was hiding. Laura quickened her step, but by the time she reached the white weatherboard house, Mrs. Murphy had gone inside and there was no sign of movement.

Laura turned to continue up the hill, then stopped and took a deep breath. After all, Mrs. Murphy had said she enjoyed talking with her and had given her the tomatoes. Surely she wouldn't mind if Laura knocked on her door. She pushed the gate open and walked down the path.

It was Leon who answered her knock. Laura shifted uncomfortably, remembering their last conversation.

"Is your grandmother at home?" she asked.

"Yes. She's always at home." But Leon did not move or call out to Mrs. Murphy. He just stood there, holding the door ajar, waiting. He looked as though he was protecting someone or something. Laura could see the heavy curtain behind him, concealing the end of the hallway, and an old wicker stand with a large plant on it.

She wondered if it was a day for people to half-open doors and stare at her, and wished she had not come. "Well, can I speak to her?" she said.

Leon's eyes narrowed. "Why?"

"Because I want to ask her something."

Leon hesitated, then stepped aside. Laura could see that he was uneasy about her coming into the house. He pulled back the curtain and led the way down the hall to a room at the end.

It was a sort of sun-room, although very little sun was coming through the louver windows, many of which had shelves stacked in front of them. It was long and narrow, and against the wall there was a large table with two chairs drawn up to one end. Mrs. Murphy was sitting in one of them, shelling peas, and Leon had obviously been sitting in the other, doing homework. His books were spread across the table and, despite the chaos, it looked companionable.

"Hello, Mrs. Murphy," said Laura, standing stiffly in the doorway.

Leon shifted some boxes from another chair and moved it next to Laura. "She says she has a question for you," he told his grandmother.

Laura was not at all sure that she wanted to ask the question anymore, particularly with Leon looking so sulky, but there was nothing else she could do now so she plunged in.

"I've just been to see Miss McInnes. I wanted to ask her about Mr. Visconti and our house. One of the librarians told me that Miss McInnes might know something about Mr. Visconti but . . . but she didn't seem very keen to talk to me. I wondered if you could help." Laura paused, considering how to phrase her request, then continued. "Do you have any suggestions about how I should approach her? I thought maybe you knew her."

"And so I do," answered Mrs. Murphy. "We were in the same grade at school. Used to play together in Mr. Gray's old quarry on Saturday afternoons. You wouldn't think it, would you, to see her now. We used to make mud pies in the dirt. She didn't mind getting grubby then." Mrs. Murphy chuckled. "The cleanliness came later. Although I must admit, her mother was always on the particular side. Used to get awfully cross with her when she came home with stained clothes and mud all over her shoes. So what do you want from her?"

"Information about the house. About Mr. Visconti."

Mrs. Murphy reached for another handful of peas. "All right, I'll see what I can do."

"I know something," said Leon unexpectedly.

Laura turned to him in surprise. "What?"

"Mr. Visconti is not buried here."

"What do you mean?"

"There's no grave for him at the cemetery."

Laura stared at him. "Maybe he was cremated," she said crossly. Mr. Visconti belonged to her. Why was Leon so interested?

"He wouldn't have been cremated back then, would he, Grandma?"

"Unlikely," said Mrs. Murphy. "Him being Italian and probably Catholic and all." She swept the empty shells into a plastic bag.

Laura frowned. "Well, how do you know he's not buried in the cemetery then?" she asked Leon.

"I looked."

Laura's mouth dropped open. "Why?"

Leon shrugged. "I was just walking past and thought I'd have a look. See what it said on his gravestone, since we'd been talking about him. But it wasn't there. It wasn't anywhere."

"There was some talk about why he lived alone,"

mused Mrs. Murphy. "I don't recall what it was — I was only a child — but there was some sort of mystery. A tragedy, I think." She frowned, as though trying to remember more. "Maybe Janet will know."

"Janet?" Laura asked.

"Janet McInnes. Come back in a few days. I might have some more information then."

"Thank you, Mrs. Murphy," said Laura, getting up. "Thank you very much."

"Don't thank me yet." Mrs. Murphy smiled as she settled back into her chair. "Wait until I have something for you. Take Laura out the back door, Leon. It's friendlier."

On the back step, Laura and Leon stood watching each other uneasily.

"Well, see you, then," said Leon.

Laura twisted her finger through her hair, thinking. If she asked Leon over, surely no one would know. How could they? It wasn't as though any kids from school lived near them. Finally, she said, "You could come and see Mr. Visconti's house, if you'd like."

"When?"

"Whenever you want, one night after school."

Laura flicked her hair back and turned to leave.

"Maybe I'll come on Monday," he called after her.

*Well, it is only fair,* thought Laura as she trudged up the hill. *After all, I barged into his house. It wouldn't be right not to let him into mine. . . .*

# ✦ CHAPTER 10 ✦

Laura spent Saturday immersed in her investigations into Mr. Visconti. Early Saturday morning she snatched a brief moment when her father wasn't working on his article to search the Internet. But while she uncovered a vast amount of information about all sorts of people named Visconti, there was nothing about *her* Mr. Visconti — nothing that she could find, anyway.

Thwarted, she returned to searching the house. She combed all the empty upstairs rooms and then climbed back into the attic to rummage through the boxes, hoping to find another postcard or maybe even a photograph. All she found, however, was an old button, a tatty brush, and another box of cutlery. In the garden she unearthed some old bottles and a few bits of broken china.

"What have you got there?" asked her mother as Laura curled up on the sofa in the studio with a large shoe box.

"My collection of things about Mr. Visconti," replied Laura.

Her mother smiled. "It looks like you've found quite a lot."

"No." Laura shook her head. "The box is mostly empty. Mr. Visconti didn't leave very much behind."

"Well, he left the house," said her mother.

Laura's brow wrinkled. "But *it* can't talk. It can't tell me about Mr. Visconti."

"Maybe it can."

Laura looked skeptical.

While her mother continued chiseling, Laura took out all the articles she had photocopied and glued them into a notebook, making notes as she went along. She soon discovered, however, that most of the notes were questions. Why did Mr. Visconti come to Australia? Why did he build the house? And why did he stay?

When Laura had finished, she thought about what her mother had said and went back to searching the house. The only other things she found, though, were a small box of paints and two thin brushes. She put them with her collection but felt rather discouraged. How did she know that any of these objects belonged to Mr. Visconti? And even if they did, what did they tell her? Nothing! She pushed the shoe box aside and picked up the novel she was reading, but she could not concentrate. All day her thoughts kept turning back to Mr. Visconti and the house.

Laura woke on Sunday to the sun streaming in her window. It was going to be a glorious day. She bounced into the kitchen and found her father sitting at the table with Samson curled up in his lap.

"It is a true sun day," he greeted her cheerfully, buttering a piece of toast. "What are you planning to do, Laura?"

"I'm going to sketch the house," she replied.

It was the little, battered box of paints that had given her the idea. As she had been drifting off to sleep, she had remembered them and wondered if Mr. Visconti had been a painter. And then she had thought that it would be fun to do some paintings of the house. Her mother always said that you got to see something differently when you drew or painted it.

She collected some sheets of paper and a box of

pencils from the studio and went out into the garden to start drawing. It proved much harder than she had imagined, however, and she was almost crying with frustration when her mother came out to see how she was doing.

"It doesn't look right. It doesn't look like the house at all," Laura complained, squinting at the lines on the paper.

Her mother took up a pencil. "Yes, it does. You just need some more shading here and a bit more height with the roof."

Laura gazed at the transformed picture. "How did you do that?" she marveled. "It looks fantastic."

"Practice." Her mother kissed her on the top of her head. "Now you try again."

When she had finished several views of the house, Laura did some drawings of the garden. She even went back up to the attic to get a bird's-eye perspective. By the end of the day, she was able to add several sketches to her Mr. Visconti box. She was very proud of them, but as she closed the lid, she thought how little she had really discovered. Mr. Visconti's story was still as mysterious as ever.

When her alarm rang on Monday morning, Laura switched it off and lay cuddled under her comforter, staring at her Mr. Visconti box, puzzling about what to do next in her investigation. Suddenly, she remembered that Leon Murphy might come over that afternoon. Perhaps he would have some ideas, but did she want to ask him? She rolled over. This was *her* mystery, and she wasn't sure she wanted to share it with anyone.

Laura glanced back at the clock. It was almost eight o'clock; she really should be getting up. She stretched, expecting to feel Samson snuggled at the bottom of her bed, but he was not there. There was not even an indentation in her comforter where he usually slept.

She jumped up, deciding that he must already be in the kitchen, waiting for his breakfast, and listened for his outraged mewing as she came down the hall. But the only sounds she heard were the hum of the fridge and the chirping of a bird in the bushes outside. Hoping he wasn't the cause of the bird's distress, she flung open the back door, but Samson wasn't in the garden either. He was nowhere to be seen.

"I'm sure he'll turn up soon," mumbled her father

sleepily when she burst into her parents' bedroom to tell them that Samson was missing. "You know what cats are like. They have their secrets."

Laura shook him. "Samson *always* comes for breakfast. He wouldn't miss it."

"Maybe he dined on mice during the night," suggested her mother. "I'm sure he's fine."

"But what if he's not fine? What if he's lying hurt somewhere, calling for us? What if he's lost?"

"We'll look for him when we get up," said her father. "You need to get ready for school."

Laura scowled and left the room, but she did not get dressed. She continued searching frantically until it was almost half past eight. It was only when she heard her father stirring that she threw on her uniform and dashed out the door without having eaten breakfast.

Halfway through her first class, Laura was starving. She looked across irritably at Leon, who was sitting on his own as usual, his eyes fixed on his textbook. Laura gnawed her fingernails. Why had she asked him over? What on earth had she been thinking? She jabbed her pen into her notebook, hoping he had forgotten all about it.

She hoped this even more fervently when she passed Kylie and Janie coming out of class.

"Leon Murphy still looking out for you?" jeered Kylie. "He must really like you."

Janie laughed. "Maybe the note was for him."

Laura hurried on. She must have been crazy to ask Leon over — what would happen if anyone saw them together now? She shuddered. Perhaps if she left immediately after school, she might make it home before him. Perhaps, then, he wouldn't come.

She dashed out as soon as the last bell rang, but when she arrived at Mrs. Murphy's cottage, Leon was sitting on the front steps, waiting for her, his bag beside him. Laura glanced around to check that no one else was nearby.

"Did you mean what you said about seeing your house?" he asked, coming up to the front gate.

"Yes," replied Laura. After all, she *had* asked him.

"Then I'll come now. I'll just dump my bag inside.

Do you want to wait?"

"All right." Laura stood uncomfortably by the fence, hoping that no one would appear. She tried to imagine what Leon would make of Mr. Visconti's house. It was so different from Mrs. Murphy's cottage.

As she watched him walk toward her, however, she realized that she was interested in his reaction. At least she felt certain he would not make jokes about ghosts and spooks. But then she remembered Samson, and a little pang of anxiety shot through her. Would he have appeared by now? She didn't know what she would do if he hadn't.

To take her mind off Samson, Laura tried to decide how much of the house she would show Leon. The studio and the murals? Surely that would be enough; she didn't need to show him anything else. She glanced sideways. Leon was so quiet, just walking along, staring at nothing in particular. She supposed that she would have to offer him a snack, but would there be anything suitable in the cupboard? Her parents had probably forgotten to do the shopping, as usual. Then she remembered a recipe for pancakes that Harry had once shown her. If all else failed, she could try making that.

At the gate Leon stopped, looking up at the house and

the monkey puzzle tree in front of it. "It's big, isn't it?"

Laura could not tell if this was a statement or a criticism. "It's not as big as it looks," she said defensively.

"It's big when you're used to a tiny apartment."

"But you don't live in a—" She stopped just in time, realizing that his father probably did. She watched him anxiously but Leon did not appear to have heard. He was still gazing up at the house, his expression inscrutable.

Laura pushed the gate open and led the way into the garden. It was heavily scented with freesias and lilacs. The fruit trees were struggling into blossom, too, white petals opening on the gnarled branches, and there were a few roses still clinging to the old bushes. The grass around them had gone to seed, and the garden beds were full of weeds.

Leon drew a deep breath and said, seemingly to himself rather than to Laura, "Wow."

"In the library there are photographs of the garden not long after it was planted," said Laura. "It was very neat then, very new."

"Imagine planning it all," replied Leon. "Thinking about what it would look like long after you're gone. Grandma always says a garden is a very hopeful thing."

"I don't suppose Mr. Visconti imagined it looking like this," said Laura.

"But I like it like this."

"So do I." Laura smiled at him. She liked that he liked the garden as it was.

As she led Leon around the side of the house and under the trellis to the kitchen door, Laura looked around for Samson. He usually appeared from the garden when she arrived home from school, stretching sleepily and mewing for the small snack that he was not supposed to have (but often did). Her heart sank when he did not come; it sank further when she realized that he was not in the kitchen either. She longed to go and look for him but instead took two glasses from the cupboard for Leon and herself. In the pantry she found a box of cookies and decided she would make the pancakes later, if it seemed appropriate.

Leon had not said anything when they entered the kitchen, but Laura could see that he was fascinated; his eyes examined everything. As she put the cookies on a plate, he went over to the window and ran his hand over the solid wooden ledge.

"If I designed a house," he said, "I would put in windows like this."

"Would you like to design houses?" asked Laura,

watching him with interest. Was this one of the secrets he had spoken of?

Leon turned and looked at her, considering. "Yes," he answered at last.

Laura felt somehow as though she had been judged and passed the test. "What sort of houses?"

"All sorts. Houses that would be fun to live in. Wild houses." He paused, frowning. "Mathematical houses."

"This is not a mathematical house." Laura gave a wry smile. "None of the windows sit right in their frames. That's why the rain comes in."

Leon turned back to the windowsill. "I didn't mean it like that."

This time Laura felt that she had failed the test. *It's like walking on shifting sand with Leon,* she thought, and changed the subject. "Would you like some juice?"

"Yes, thank you." He had become very formal.

While Laura was concentrating on pouring the drinks, her father came into the room. He was in a disheveled state, hair falling over his forehead, holes in his sweater and stains on his jeans. There were dark shadows under his eyes, and when he looked at Leon, it was as though he was trying to focus. Laura knew it was because he had been working all day and most of last night on an article with another tight deadline. She wondered if she should explain this to Leon, but he did not seem disconcerted.

"Hello, Mr. Horton," he said politely.

"This is Leon Murphy." Laura turned to her father, waiting for his eyes to clear. "Has Samson turned up?"

"Sorry, sweetheart, but I'm sure he will soon."

Laura swallowed. She knew something was wrong. If she had stayed home, she would have found him by now.

"Who is Samson?" asked Leon.

"My cat. He's disappeared." She tried not to panic. "Leon has come to look at the house," she said to her father, attempting to make her voice sound as normal as possible. She did not want to talk about Samson in front of Leon.

"Understandably. It's a very good house to look at," replied her father, smiling at Leon.

"Remember I told you his grandmother knew Mr. Visconti? Or at least she saw him when she was little."

Her father nodded. "He must have been an

interesting person," he said. "I like what I know of him, from the traces he left."

"How's the article going?" asked Laura, still trying to get the image of a bedraggled, frightened Samson out of her mind.

"Finished, thank God. Sent off—and ten minutes before it was due. Would you like a cookie, Leon? I think they're all right but you never can tell with things in our pantry."

"They're all right," confirmed Laura. "I tried one."

"Very noble of you, putting your stomach at risk like that." Her father grinned and ruffled her hair. "Well, Leon, the official food taster says they're fine. Are you willing to risk one?"

Leon took a cookie.

"Come and see the ballroom," said Laura. "My mom will be there."

They went out into the hall, and then Leon stopped abruptly. "What's that?" he asked, tilting his head to one side.

"What?"

"Listen." From high above came a tiny meow. It was only just audible.

"It's coming from the attic," Laura cried. "I went

up there yesterday. Why didn't I think of it before? Samson must have followed me up and been shut in."

She dashed out into the entrance area and up the wide staircase, Leon following.

"He must be feeling desperate," she gasped as they reached the attic.

Leon grinned. "He sounds more cross than anything else."

When she opened the door, a small furry head appeared, covered in cobwebs. As Laura gathered him into her arms, Samson explained in loud, emphatic mews that he was terribly, terribly upset—and terribly, terribly hungry. They carried him downstairs and gave him two dinners and a bowl of milk, and his purrs were so loud they filled the whole kitchen.

Laura looked up at Leon. "If you hadn't heard him, he might have died," she said, stroking Samson's gray fur.

"You would have heard him," replied Leon.

But Laura was not so sure. She smiled at Leon, feeling suddenly very friendly toward him. "Come, I'll show you the ballroom."

# ✦ CHAPTER 11 ✦

Laura's mother was leaning over the plan press, working on a sketch, when Laura and Leon came into the studio. The radio was on, and she was humming along to Bob Dylan as her hand moved across the page.

"Hello, honey bear," she said, glancing up. Then she caught sight of Leon, lagging behind Laura, and put down her stick of charcoal.

"Mom, this is Leon Murphy. We found Samson."

Laura's mother smiled. "Hello, Leon. That's wonderful news, Laura. I told you he'd turn up."

"He didn't turn up. Leon heard him. He was in the attic. He might have died!"

"Not with all the mice around. Still, he would have been lonely until we found him—and you would have been very miserable—so I must thank you, Leon, for rescuing our errant feline and saving us from that fate. It's very nice to meet you. We don't often get to meet Laura's friends."

Leon coughed awkwardly, and Laura blushed.

"Leon has come to look at the house," she said.

"It's a wonderful old place, isn't it?" replied her mother. "We've made a bit of a mess of this room, I'm afraid, but the bones are still here. It must have been very grand."

Leon's eyes swept the room, taking in the half-finished sculpture in the center, the stone and metal stacked against the walls, the ceiling soaring above them, and the tall French windows looking out to the wild garden beyond. "It's amazing," he said.

"Do you think that Mr. Visconti held balls in here?" asked Laura.

"No." Leon's voice was firm.

Laura looked at him in surprise. She hadn't expected him to have an opinion. "Why not? How can you be so sure?"

"Because my grandmother says she doesn't remember anyone coming to the house."

Laura considered this. "Maybe he held balls when he was younger," she said. "He was already old when your grandmother was a little girl."

"Maybe, but she doesn't remember anyone talking about balls and things. She said that everyone said he always lived very quietly, very privately.

That was why people knew so little about him."

"But why would he build a ballroom if he wasn't going to use it?" protested Laura.

"Perhaps he thought he would use it and then something happened."

Laura frowned. She did not want to let go of everything she had imagined. She had seen women, resplendent in silk and lace, swirling around the room in the arms of elegant young men. She had heard the strains of music drifting out into the candlelit garden and seen musicians, dressed all in black, drawing their bows across their polished violins.

"I think there were balls," she insisted stubbornly. "Lots of them. And parties. I think there were carriages coming up from Melbourne, full of people, but they must have come late at night when your grandmother was in bed."

"I don't think so," said Leon.

Laura's mother smiled at them both. "You can each hold on to your own ideas," she said. "I guess we'll never know."

"But I want to know," replied Laura.

"Even if there were no parties?" asked Leon.

"Yes. I want to know what he was doing here and why." She tilted her head back, gazing up to the ceiling soaring above them. "It's so strange to think that he lived here in these rooms, that he decorated them and walked through them and slept in them, and we know nothing about him."

Leon looked at her with his considering expression. "Maybe we will find out," he said after a pause. "Where are the paintings?"

"In here." Laura led the way back through the hall, and Leon followed after a quick, polite nod to her mother. The curtains in the bedroom were still drawn, and in the half light the large bed appeared to fill the whole room.

Leon stared at it, his mouth dropping open. "Was that here when you moved in?"

"No. My mom made it."

Leon ran his hand down one of the turned posts. "It's really good," he said. "It's not like the other things she makes, is it? I mean the other things are good too, but they're very different from this."

Laura laughed. "This is furniture. The other things are art."

"Is that what your mom says?"

"Yes. She made it because she said the room needed a four-poster bed. She can make almost anything, like beds and sculptures. She can't make food, though. She says so herself," added Laura, in case Leon thought she was being disloyal. "What about your mom? What does she do?"

"My mom is dead," said Leon.

"Oh, I didn't . . ." stuttered Laura, stricken. "I'm sorry, I . . ." She stopped, not knowing how to continue.

Leon turned away. "There's just Dad and me—and Grandma. Are those the paintings?" He nodded toward the wall.

Laura looked at him diffidently. She wanted to say something more, to say how awful that was and how sorry she was, but Leon had gone over to the wall and was peering at the faint images. From the way he had turned so abruptly, she knew that he didn't want to talk about it.

"Yes," she replied. "What's left of them." Laura pulled back the curtains and light flooded in. It illuminated the unmade bed, the scattered books, the piles of clothes, and fell across one wall where dark patches of paint still suggested an Italianate garden with trees, the top of a fountain, and the remains of sweeping steps. Leon squinted at it.

"That's the best bit," said Laura, coming over to him. "But there are some trees over there too, and part of a hedge."

"I wonder who painted it," murmured Leon. "It's awesome."

"It must have been wonderful when the whole room was a garden," said Laura.

"Yes. Like stepping into a dream." Leon lightly touched the painted surface. "Did you find any photos of this room when you went to the library?"

"How did you know that was what I was doing at the library?" Laura asked.

"I just guessed. Did you?"

Laura shook her head. "No, there were no pictures of the inside of the house at all, only the outside."

"Have you tried the Internet?"

"Of course. There was heaps and heaps of stuff about people named Visconti, but nothing about our Mr. Visconti."

It wasn't until the words were out that Laura realized what she had said. She had called him *our Mr. Visconti*—as though Mr. Visconti belonged to Leon, too.

Leon leaned forward to examine the painting more

closely. "I could help you look for things, information, if you'd like."

"I've looked at everything." Laura shrugged. "There isn't anything more to find."

"You don't know. There may be." Leon was tracing one of the trees with his finger. "Different people look at things differently."

Laura hesitated. Leon was not like anyone else she had met. She liked talking to him, and it could be fun looking for Mr. Visconti together—after all, she thought again, who would ever find out?

"All right," she said, then added, "Would you like to see the other rooms?"

Leon grinned. "What do you think?"

They ended up going through the whole house together, even the empty sections with their crumbling plaster and dust and grime. Leon climbed over the boxes in the sheds, fingered the old, rotting curtains, and looked out of every window. To Laura, he seemed to be making lists in his mind. Lists of what he was seeing, or maybe of what he wanted to remember. Perhaps it was because he saw everything in a mathematical way, she reflected.

Laura discovered that it was more intriguing

exploring the house with someone else, someone her own age. It had been fun in the attic with Isabella, but this was fun in a completely different way. It was like looking at the house with someone who was the same height, who saw things from the same angle—although differently, which was what made it interesting.

Leon was so enthusiastic, she even told him some of the stories she had imagined in the different rooms. "This," she said, leaning out the window of a small upper room, "is like an aerie, like a tower room. It looks out over the world. You could imagine a servant coming here, escaping in her dreams, couldn't you? She would have so little time and be so tired but, for a moment, from this window, she could fly away."

Leon leaned out too, narrowing his eyes as he looked past the fruit trees to the dusty hill beyond. Laura watched him reach out to touch the rough wall and then turn back to the dark room. He seemed to touch everything, she thought.

Finally, he replied. "It would be hard for your servant to return."

"A little harder each time," she agreed. "Maybe one day she doesn't."

"It's a good story. You should write it down."

Laura thought of the little pieces of paper

fluttering to the desk in the stuffy, closed classroom and of her dragon book, which she could no longer write. She wondered how much Leon had actually guessed about her.

"It's just a story," she said. "Let's go downstairs."

The kitchen was empty when they returned. Laura's parents were still busy working and, although it was almost dinnertime, there was no sign of dinner. After all their exploring, Laura was famished. "Would you like some pancakes?" she asked Leon.

Leon raised his eyebrows. "Pancakes?"

"Yes." Laura suddenly felt rather silly. "You don't have to have any."

"No, I'd like some. I was just surprised."

"Why?"

"It seems a bit late to have pancakes. When do you usually eat?"

Laura shrugged. "Whenever someone cooks dinner."

"That sounds like my dad." Leon looked around. "Where are the pancakes?"

"I'm going to make them." Laura hesitated. "Will your grandmother care when you get back?"

"No. She knows that I'm here."

The pancakes turned out well; Laura was proud of them. While they were cooking, she showed Leon her book with the photocopied articles and her box of information about Mr. Visconti, leaving him to pore over them while she tried, not always successfully, to flip the pancakes in the pan. Fortunately, there was butter and jam in the fridge. She wondered whether to just put the containers on the table but decided, in the end, to do it properly and scooped the jam into a bowl and cut a slab of butter for the butter dish. Then, remembering Isabella, she moved a vase of forget-me-nots onto the table.

"The pancakes smell good," said Leon, looking up.

"You can start. I've almost finished."

"No, I'll wait."

Leon had been leafing through the book. He stopped at an article from 1898 and pointed to one of the paragraphs. "This is interesting—this bit about the visiting singer."

Laura leaned over his shoulder, the frying pan suspended in the air beside her, to see what he was referring to. "Yes, it says that the singer stayed with Mr. Visconti and gave a concert here in this house."

"So he must have been sociable once, despite what Grandma remembers," said Leon. "Do you think the concert was held in the ballroom?"

"Maybe. Or maybe in the painted room. Perhaps it was a music room."

"It would make a good music room."

"Yes. With a grand piano and everyone dressed in beautiful clothes and the Italian tenor singing among the painted trees. It would have been wonderful." Laura sighed, thinking again of Isabella. "I wish there was a picture of it."

"I wonder what the people in the town thought of it all. Pretty strange, I imagine."

"They always think everything different is strange," said Laura bitterly.

Leon looked up at her for a moment, his expression once again inscrutable, then went back to reading the newspaper article.

When the pancakes were ready, Laura cut up a small one and put it in Samson's bowl. He ran over and sniffed at it. She then put the others on a plate, and for a while they concentrated on eating, although Leon continued to flip through the book. When most of the pancakes were gone, he turned his attention to the box. The first things he noticed were Laura's sketches of the house.

"I like these." He looked up at her and grinned. "Your perspective is a bit odd, though."

Laura made a face at him, but strangely she did not feel offended.

Then Leon caught sight of the postcard. "What's this?" he asked, picking it up. He studied the picture of the wide street with its tall palms and elegant people, then turned it over to look at the writing on the back.

"What language do you think it is?" asked Laura.

"Italian, maybe," suggested Leon, staring down at it. "Yes, I think it's Italian."

"Can you read it?"

"No." Leon continued to study it. "If it's Italian, my dad could, though."

"Would he translate it for us?" asked Laura tentatively, remembering how he had reacted the last time she mentioned his father.

"Of course. Where did you find it?"

"On the floor of the attic. Perhaps it fell out of a trunk or a box that was stored there."

"Perhaps." Leon was studying the stamp. "But this is not Italian," he said. "It's a French stamp."

He turned the postcard over and looked again at the boulevard. "It looks like the south of France."

"Have you been there?" asked Laura, her mouth full of pancake.

"Of course not." Leon raised his eyebrows at her.

She frowned. "Then how do you know it's the south of France?"

"I didn't say I knew. I just said it looks like the south of France. I've seen pictures of Nice and they have palm trees, just like this. And there's a French stamp."

"Maybe the words will tell us something," said Laura.

"There's no signature. Just a *G*. And the address has been smudged. I can't read it. Can you?"

Laura shook her head. "That could be a name," she suggested, pointing to a word at the end of the second line. "Alessandro."

"Maybe it's a place. Alexandria?"

They both stared at it for a while, then Leon turned back to Laura's book. He found the page where she had copied information from an obituary.

"His name was Carlo," he said.

"There's definitely no Carlo on the postcard. Nothing that even looks like *Carlo*." Laura was still gazing intently at the writing on the card. "If it *is* in Italian, though, it must have been written to Mr. Visconti."

"Maybe." Leon took another pancake and looked across at Laura. "So, what do we know for sure about Mr. Visconti? We know that he was Italian and that he came to Australia, probably in 1894. We know that he built this house and lived in it and invited a singer to perform in it and that he died, probably in 1938, and is not buried in the graveyard here."

"We know that he went for walks."

"And we know the house. I mean, what the house is like. It tells us something about him — that he liked gardens, for example, and art."

"And that he was rich," added Laura.

"Yes. I wonder what he was rich from."

"One article says that he was a diplomat." Laura flipped through the pages, looking for it.

"I don't think diplomats make that much money," said Leon. "Not enough to build this in the 1890s, at any rate."

"Maybe he already had money. Maybe he came from an old aristocratic family."

"Who?" asked Laura's mother, coming into the kitchen.

"Mr. Visconti," replied Laura. "But why did he settle here?"

Laura's mother buttered a pancake and bit into it. "Mmm, these are delicious," she said, sitting down. "Imagine me having a daughter who is a good cook." She smiled at Laura and started buttering another pancake. "Maybe there was a love affair."

Laura stared at her in amazement. "What kind of love affair?" she said.

"The usual kind. Perhaps it ended tragically."

Laura was thinking furiously. "But of course," she muttered, "that would explain everything."

"Not everything," said Leon.

"Well, lots of things." Leon nodded in agreement. Laura continued to look at him, her brow furrowed in concentration. "Perhaps that was why he came out here."

"And maybe she died," added Leon.

Suddenly, there was a chill in the air.

"I should be going." Leon pushed back his chair. "It's getting late. Thank you for the pancakes, Laura. Would it be all right if I take the postcard?"

Laura nodded. "I'll come to the gate with you."

The sun was setting, and the bushes along the driveway threw long shadows across the path as they walked down it. Samson appeared from his favorite flower bed, mewing, and Leon picked him up. When he tickled him under his chin, Samson purred and Laura laughed. She realized that her afternoon with Leon had been really enjoyable. She was glad he had come.

"Should we go to the library tomorrow and look at the papers again?" asked Leon. "I'd really like to see the photos there."

Laura gulped. This would mean going into town with Leon; when she had said he could help her look for information about Mr. Visconti, that was not what she had meant. She felt Leon's eyes on her face and had the uneasy sensation that he was reading her thoughts.

"All right," she said quickly. "I'll meet you there after school."

"OK." Leon thrust his hands into his pockets and wandered off, unhurried.

Laura turned back toward the house. She looked up at the dark monkey puzzle tree with its spiky leaves clustered along its thin branches, biting her lip. Someone was sure to see them in the library. What would they think?

⁕ CHAPTER 12 ⁕

Laura was careful to leave very early the next morning so that she would not bump into Leon. While she didn't mind him coming to the house and she was prepared to meet him at the library, she did not want to be seen walking to school with him. She could just imagine what Kylie and Maddy would say then—if she arrived at school with Leon Murphy, she would simply never live it down.

When Leon did not turn up for their first class, however, Laura felt rather disappointed, and as the day drifted on and he still did not appear, she realized that she was quite deflated. She had been looking forward to showing him Mr. Visconti's photographs in the library after school. When classes finished for the day, she wondered whether to head straight home—after all, he was probably sick with a cold—but a niggling feeling of responsibility made her go to the library first, just to check. As soon as she walked in, she saw Leon, sitting at a table by the window with the file on Mr. Visconti open in front of him.

Laura felt cross. Why didn't he tell her that he would be away? She hesitated for a moment, then approached him. "So where were you?" she asked coldly.

"I went down to Melbourne to see my dad."

"Oh." Laura sat down, her anger suddenly gone. "Just like that. Didn't he mind you missing school?"

Leon did not reply; he shrugged his shoulders and looked out the window.

"Well, could he translate the postcard?" she said impatiently.

"Yes, I told you he could."

"And?"

Leon drew a piece of paper from his pocket and handed it to Laura.

"'The sea is calm today,'" she read. "'No more storms. I saw Alessandro yesterday, and he told me about the painted garden. I long to see it. I long to see you, but there is too much sea between us. When will you return? G.'"

"Gosh," breathed Laura. "Who do you think *G* is?"

Leon shrugged his shoulders again. "Could be anybody."

"It sounds like it was someone who knew Mr. Visconti well."

"*If* the postcard was for Mr. Visconti." Leon raised one eyebrow. "Who knows?"

"Of course it was for Mr. Visconti. Why else would it be in his house? In the *attic* of his house? And he had been away many years, so of course people would long to see him. And the garden, the *painted* garden." Laura pointed to the words. "You are just being difficult."

"Perhaps." Leon grinned at her. "I admit that it probably was for him. My dad said that the picture *is* a photograph of Nice."

"Maybe Alessandro is the person who painted the garden."

"Maybe. Or maybe he was the singer who gave the concert."

Laura's face lit up. "Yes, that would be who he was. The singer's initial was *A*, I'm sure. Where's the article?" She started rummaging through the papers.

"Here," said Leon.

He had been looking at it when she arrived.

Laura stared at him in disbelief. Leon had to be the most frustrating person she knew. "You might have told me you'd already figured it out. Show me the clipping again."

Laughing, Leon handed it to her, and Laura began to read. "'A well-known singer, A. Bernascotti from Rome, has been staying with Mr. Visconti. On September 9, 1898, he gave a concert at Mr. Visconti's charming residence. It was greatly enjoyed by all who attended. Items included . . .'" Laura looked up. "The songs sound like the sort of things Isabella used to sing."

"Who was Isabella?"

"Is, not was. She's a friend of my parents. She wants to be an opera singer." Laura remembered all the arias and smiled. "She said our house was made to sing in."

"Maybe it was."

Laura returned to the browning newspaper clipping. "Do you think that *G* is a man or a woman?" she asked.

"I don't think that *G* is the person in the love affair, if that's what you're suggesting."

"Why not?"

"It just doesn't sound like that to me. And I don't think it would have been dropped on the floor for people to find one hundred years later if it was."

"How do you know?"

"I don't know—but it's what I think. I think that *G* was someone who knew Mr. Visconti well but was not his . . ." Leon blushed slightly. "Not the person he was in love with."

"And who *was* he in love with?"

"The person he built the house for."

Of course; how could she have been so blind? It was so obvious—Mr. Visconti had not built the house for himself. He had built it for someone else. For someone he loved.

"Maybe Miss McInnes knows who she is," she suggested. "When do you think your grandmother will talk to her?"

"She said she was waiting until the time was right."

"And what does that mean?"

"It means she's waiting until she feels up to it. She doesn't like going out."

Laura wrinkled her forehead. "It's funny, isn't it, to think of her and Miss McInnes playing in the school yard, being children?"

"It's funny thinking of most adults being children," agreed Leon. "What's Miss McInnes like?"

"Very neat and ordered. An everything-in-its-place

sort of person, I think. And suspicious. Well, she was suspicious of me, anyway."

Leon grinned again. "Maybe you looked shady." he said. "Look at this description of the house. It says there was a cellar."

"But there isn't," replied Laura. "I would have shown it to you if there was. When was that written?"

"In 1940, when the house was up for sale. It says that there had once been a well-stocked cellar."

Laura slowly shook her head. "I've never seen it."

"That doesn't mean it isn't there. Or *wasn't* there. It may have been covered over. We should look for it."

"I guess we could try to find it." Laura eyed the article skeptically. "Does it say where it was?"

"No."

"Well, do you want to come over tomorrow after school? We could search for it then."

"Sure." Leon nodded, but as though he had not really heard. He turned toward her, a puzzled expression on his face. "Strange that the cellar's not there anymore, isn't it? Really, really strange."

## CHAPTER 13

The following afternoon, Leon was sitting on the balustrade of Mrs. Murphy's veranda, eating an apple, when Laura came over the hill. He leaped down as soon as he saw her, and she could tell immediately that he had some news.

"Your mom was right," he blurted out as he reached her. "There *was* a romance. Mr. Visconti met this woman. He came out to Australia because he wanted to marry her. He built your house for her and everything, but something went wrong. She never married him. He went on living there, waiting, but she never came."

Laura put down her bag, frowning as she tried to take it all in. "But why did he build it here?"

"She lived nearby. Her family had a property, a big property. Her father was very rich. She met Mr. Visconti when she was on the Grand Tour, traveling all over Europe, becoming a lady."

"So why didn't she marry him?"

"I don't know. Miss McInnes didn't say."

"*Wouldn't* say?"

"No, Grandma thinks she doesn't know. Remember, she was only a little girl when she heard all this. Miss McInnes was related to the family, very distantly; that's how she knew about it. But there was some sort of scandal and it was all hushed up. Maybe it was because the family didn't approve of Mr. Visconti. Because he was Italian. Or because he was different."

"Because he built houses with gardens painted on the walls."

"Maybe."

Laura was silent for a moment, then said, "People are so stupid."

"Only some." Leon took another bite of his apple. "Come on. Let's get going."

Laura bent to pick up her bag, but Leon seized it from her. "Here, I'll carry that," he said, and swung it over his shoulder as though it weighed nothing. Laura stared after him in surprise. She had read about boys carrying girls' school books in some of her mother's old novels, but she hadn't imagined that they really did it. Not that this was like in the stories, she reminded herself—he was just carrying it because it was heavy —but it was nice all the same. She hurried to catch up with him.

Laura's mother was making coffee when they came into the kitchen. She smiled at Leon and asked how their research was going.

"Fine," said Laura. "We're going to look for a cellar."

"A cellar! Why?"

"One of the articles said there was a cellar."

Laura's mother shook her head. "You can't believe everything you read, you know. I haven't seen any evidence of a cellar, honey bear."

"Well, we're going to see for ourselves." Laura opened the fridge and then closed it again when she saw they were all out of juice. She didn't think Leon was the sort of person who would mind about things like that, though. "Would you like some water?" she asked, but he shook his head.

"There's some fresh bread," suggested her mother. "Your father came back with a loaf when he went to get the paper. And there's that delicious honey Harry brought. Why don't you have some of that?"

The bread was so fresh, it was hard to cut. They ended up with huge wedges on which they slathered butter and the sweet golden honey. It dribbled over the sides and stuck to their fingers and tasted incredible. Watching Leon as he licked the side of his hand where the honey was trickling down, Laura tried to imagine eating bread and honey with Kylie or Maddy. It was impossible to do.

"Where should we start?" she asked when they couldn't eat any more.

"Are there any new floorboards?"

Laura thought hard. "I don't think so."

"Let's look anyway. We'll start here."

The kitchen was tiled. The tiles were old and worn and looked very firmly set in place. Nevertheless, Leon insisted that they shift every bit of movable furniture to look under it. They found nothing.

Then they tried the two bedrooms, crawling over the floorboards to check every join. At one point, after he had been peering under her parents' bed, Leon lifted his head, and he was covered in cobwebs and dust. Laura burst out laughing, and Leon, looking puzzled, reached up and felt the sticky threads caught in his hair.

"Look in the mirror." Laura giggled. "You look like Samson when we found him in the attic."

Leon started laughing too, and the more they

laughed, the more they could not stop. Laura clutched her stomach and gasped for air. When they finally managed to catch their breath, she realized she hadn't laughed like that in a very, very long time. She thought of the last night with Harry and Isabella when she had felt so lonely and miserable; perhaps she was going to end up friends with Leon, after all.

The next room they searched was the room Isabella and Laura had turned into the dining room. Samson was asleep on the table among the gutted candlesticks and the remains of Isabella's vegetable centerpiece. When they came in, he looked up sleepily and yawned, making them both start laughing again. Laura picked him up and he began to purr, rubbing his head against her neck.

Leon tickled Samson's chin. "You're so lucky to have a cat."

"Do you . . . did you have any animals?" asked Laura.

"I had a dog once." Leon turned away. "I couldn't keep him," he said in a voice that told Laura not to go any further. "Let's start looking for the cellar here."

As Laura watched him kneel down and begin to examine the boards, she wondered if he would ever tell her about himself. She put Samson down and joined Leon on the floor. Samson followed them, puzzled by their odd behavior.

"This would be a good room for a cellar because it's next to the kitchen," said Leon.

"Maybe." Laura sat back on her heels and looked around. "But I can't see where it would be. I think Mom was right. I think they were just making it up in the article." She pressed her lips together scornfully.

Leon glanced at her. "Let's keep looking anyway."

They tried the other empty rooms on the ground floor and then the hall and the grand entrance area with its marble tiles. It was getting dark by then, and the shadows were closing in. For a moment Laura almost heard the soft *tap, tap, tap* of Mr. Visconti's stick on the stone as he crossed the hall and began to mount the stairs.

She shivered. "I think we should stop now," she said. Then something caught her eye. It was glinting in the half light beside the staircase. "Look," she cried. "What's that?"

It was a key. A tiny silver key jammed beneath the baseboard.

## CHAPTER 14

The key did not seem to fit anything, but Laura and Leon put it away carefully in the Mr. Visconti box with all the other discoveries. It was so small that Laura had to find another box to keep it in. She lined this box with some silk ribbon, and when she had polished the tiny, delicately patterned key, it nestled in the folds like a jewel.

The discovery of the key convinced Laura that there was definitely more to find, and she responded enthusiastically when Leon suggested continuing their search for the cellar. "We'll carry on tomorrow," she said, but Leon shook his head.

"I can't come back till Saturday."

Laura waited for him to elaborate but he didn't.

Over the next two days, she spent a lot of time speculating about what he was doing, particularly when he did not turn up at school on either of those days. Was it something to do with his father? Or something else entirely? She was unsettled to discover that she missed seeing him around.

He arrived early on Saturday morning, while Laura and her parents were still eating breakfast. Laura jumped up as soon as she heard his footsteps on the gravel and ran to the door to meet him. She was surprised to see that he was carrying Samson, who was purring.

"I found him rolling in the road," Leon explained. "I tried to convince him it wasn't a good idea, but I'm not sure he agrees."

Laura looked severely at Samson, who purred more loudly and stretched back, rubbing his head against Leon's sleeve.

"He'd better come searching with us," she said, scratching under his collar. "We should start in the studio since Mom's not working yet."

Leon looked over her shoulder into the kitchen.

"Have I come too early?" he asked, catching sight of her parents at the table.

"No, of course not. Mom and Dad always spend forever over the weekend papers. Come in. Do you want some toast?"

Leon shook his head. He was still hovering uncertainly on the doorstep.

"Come on." Laura wondered if she would have to drag him in but, after a moment, he followed her. She snatched the half-eaten piece of toast from her plate and headed for the hall. Behind her she heard Leon saying good morning to her parents in his polite "talking to grown-ups" voice. Why was he so apprehensive?

"I hope your mom doesn't mind," he whispered as they reached the studio door.

"No, it's fine. She doesn't mind at all." Laura smiled at him reassuringly. "We can't move the stone and metal, of course, or disturb things she's working on. That won't matter, though — it's not likely anyone would put a cellar in a ballroom, is it?"

Leon put Samson down, and the cat stalked off to the center of the room where the sun was streaming in. He sat down, lifted one leg into the air, and began delicately washing himself. Laura laughed. "He's not going to be much help."

They looked everywhere but found nothing. Then they went out into the garden because Leon thought there might have been an outhouse with a cellar.

"Maybe we're looking in the wrong place," he said, running his hand through his hair.

Laura's gaze swept the yard. "You'd think there'd

be some trace of it, if it was here."

"Not if it was pulled down and the garden grew over it. At least, not a noticeable trace." Leon scuffed the grass near the back door with his foot. "Maybe it was deliberately covered up."

"But why?" demanded Laura. "Why would anyone deliberately cover it up?"

Leon dug the toe of his shoe into the ground. "Maybe the outhouse was taken down because it wasn't needed anymore. It wouldn't take long for the garden to spread. Grandma says there's no stopping a garden once it's let go."

Laura started scuffing the ground too. By mid morning there were little holes all over the garden. Laura was hot and grumpy but there was still no sign of a cellar or an outhouse. No sign of anything except dirt.

"I think it's all nonsense," she muttered. "I don't think there was ever any cellar. They just got it all mixed up in that article. They probably meant the pantry. We have one of those—let's go and find something to eat in it."

Leon followed her back into the kitchen and helped her carry some glasses to the table, but she could see that he was not thinking about the drinks or the food. His eyes had their faraway, concentrating expression.

"Leon, do you want a cookie?" she asked for a second time, pushing the plate toward him.

Leon took one without answering. "Where would you dig a cellar?" he asked.

Laura rolled her eyes. "Under the ground."

"Yes, but where under the ground?"

"Near the kitchen," she said. "Where we've been looking. Where the cellar *isn't*."

Leon frowned, ignoring the sarcasm in her voice. "So would I. So why isn't it there?"

"Because it never was, maybe?"

Leon went on staring at the untouched cookie in his hand. "It must be somewhere."

"Why are you so keen to find it? It would just be an old cellar."

"An old cellar would be a good place to hide things."

"What sort of things?" asked Laura.

"I don't know. Just things. Things you don't want to destroy but don't want anyone to see. Valuable things."

Laura sipped her drink. Was Leon ever going to admit defeat? The cellar obviously wasn't there. "So should we stop searching?"

Leon didn't reply. Laura watched him for a while, then said doubtfully, "Maybe we should look inside again. Maybe we missed something."

"No." Leon shook his head. "We've looked everywhere. We have to approach it in a different way."

Laura took another cookie and bit into it impatiently. What different way was there? They had tried everything. They sat staring at each other in silence until Laura's father came into the kitchen, still in his robe, his hair tousled and a coffee cup in his hand. "Have you given up yet?"

Laura turned to him. "If *you* were looking for a cellar, where would you look?"

He stood at the sink, rinsing the coffee infuser and deliberating. "Under the stairs," he replied at last.

"But there's nothing under the stairs. It's all boarded up. Or rather, walled up." Laura paused, then her eyes caught her father's and she flashed him a grin.

"No, categorically no." Her father shook his head. "I know it's very unexciting of me, but I don't want you hacking into the paneling under the stairs, just in case there's a cellar behind it. Things are decayed enough around here without you dismantling a wall."

"There might be priceless treasures behind it!"

"And there might not be."

Laura nudged Leon and whispered, "Let's go and look," but Leon shook his head, his eyes on Laura's father.

"It's all right." Laura raised her voice. "We're just going to look. Come on."

Her father called after them, "No dismantling, do you hear?"

"I don't know why he's so worried about it," grumbled Laura as they crossed the hall. "The whole place is crumbling anyway."

"Maybe that's what's troubling him," said Leon.

"I don't think so. He never usually thinks about it."

They stood in the entrance area, looking up at the staircase and the stained-glass window above, and Laura remembered her impression of Mr. Visconti slowly *tap, tap, tapping* his way through the shadows to the stairs.

There were no shadows now. The morning light was streaming in, illuminating the dust on the patterned floor and the scuff marks where they had been searching previously. Mr. Visconti seemed a very long way away.

Leon knocked against the paneling at the side of the staircase. "It could have been added later, I suppose." He looked dubious. "It looks pretty old to me, though."

Laura ran her hands over it. "There would have been a door," she said. "And steps behind it." She too knocked against the wood. "It sounds hollow."

Leon nodded. "But why would anyone seal it up? It doesn't make sense."

They stood staring at the wood as though they expected it to speak. Eventually, Laura said, "I wish Dad would let us pull off just one board. Then we would know if there *was* something there. It's ridiculous; they both make heaps of mess all the time. Why can't we make just a little?"

Leon looked uneasily toward the kitchen. "I guess we should leave it—"

Before he could finish, a fanfare from a horn sounded suddenly outside the house. Car doors slammed, and voices echoed down the driveway.

"It's Harry and Isabella," cried Laura, dashing out to the kitchen. "They've come back!"

## CHAPTER 15

Laura entered the kitchen in a rush and then skidded to a halt. A huge bear of a man with bushy eyebrows and an extravagant beard was towering by the door. She took a step backward and trod on Leon, who was just behind her. "This is Hugo," explained Isabella, laughing as she threw her bag onto a chair. "He's a singer, too. He knows all about you and this wonderful house. I told him it was a house to sing in and that he had to see it."

Hugo beamed at them all, and Laura, recovering, threw herself into Isabella's arms and then Harry's. "I've missed you so much," she cried.

"But we've only been gone a short time," replied Harry. He swung Laura up into the air as though she were still a little girl, and her arm knocked the herbs hanging by the pantry. "Ah, I see you've been using my garlic."

"Yes, I cooked up tomatoes and they were really

good. I crushed the garlic like you showed me, but it made my hands smell for days."

"That's the sign of a good cook." Harry nodded and winked at Laura's mother. "You have to suffer for your art, don't you, Lesley?"

"Especially when you have deadlines," she said, laughing.

Isabella threw her head back and began to sing about suffering, but stopped midnote—she had caught sight of Leon, standing in the corner, pressed against the wall.

"Who is this?" she exclaimed, waving her arms and all her bracelets toward him. Leon pressed farther back, looking desperate, and Laura felt a sudden rush of remorse. She had been so excited about Harry and Isabella arriving, she had completely forgotten Leon. She could see that he was feeling overwhelmed. It was not just shyness; it was something else. Something she could not put her finger on.

"This is Leon," she said, turning toward him. "Leon, this is Isabella, the opera singer I was telling you about."

"Leon." Isabella regarded him thoughtfully. "I'm very pleased to meet you. Now tell me all about yourself."

Leon opened his mouth and then closed it, without any sound coming out. Laura saw him dart a quick glance toward the garden, visible through the open door, almost as though he were counting the number of steps between him and his escape.

"Leon goes to school with me," she said. "We're investigating this house and the man who built it. We think we've found a cellar, but Dad won't let us look."

"Why ever not?"

"We would have to take down some paneling. He says it would make too much mess."

"Andrew," Isabella called across the room, "why not let the kids look for their cellar?"

Behind Isabella's back, Laura grinned at Leon, but he did not smile back. "They won't bite," she whispered, but he still didn't smile.

"We've got enough mess already," answered Laura's father. "Just look at the house."

"But it's beautiful," said Isabella. "And anyway, we'll help tidy up afterward, won't we, Harry?"

"I always tidy up afterward," said Harry, slightly aggrieved.

"It's not cooking, Harry." Isabella slid her arm through his. "It's taking down a wall."

Harry looked horrified. "But I don't want to take down a wall."

Laura giggled. "We do."

"And I'm saying that we'll help put it back up again," explained Isabella.

"No." Harry shook his head emphatically. "I can't put up walls."

"I can," said Hugo unexpectedly. "I will help."

Laura nudged Leon and whispered, "It's a good thing Hugo came."

Leon did not reply. He was looking at her father, who had buried his head in his hands, muttering, "I don't want any more confusion. I want order, order . . ."

"You can have order — afterward." Isabella winked at Laura. "Anyway, you don't really want order, Andrew. You just think you do. Order is boring."

"The man who built this house gave a concert in it, Isabella," said Laura. "He had singers visit. Singers like you." She turned to Leon for corroboration, but could not see him. He was behind her, edging to the door.

"I think I'd better be going," he said.

"You can't go yet." Laura grabbed his arm. "Come and we'll show Isabella where we think the cellar is."

As they walked down the hall, Laura suddenly became aware that she was still grasping Leon's arm. She dropped it quickly, flushing a little. For a moment she caught a glimpse of the old Leon, one eyebrow raised in amusement. Then Isabella approached and his face went blank.

"So where is this mysterious cellar?" asked Isabella.

"Through here." Laura pointed. "Under the stairs. All we have to do is take off some of this paneling and shine a light in. Isabella came at just the right time, didn't she, Leon?" She turned back to Leon and saw him fiddling with the neck of his T-shirt. Again, he did not reply.

Isabella laughed. "Give him time, Laura," she said. "We take a bit of getting used to. Particularly me. Why do you think there's a cellar behind this paneling?"

"We read about it in an article about the house. It was Leon who picked it up—the reference to the cellar, I mean." Laura looked back at Leon, who was now staring at his shoes as though he wasn't interested. Laura felt like shaking him. "We've been searching and searching and this is the first real possibility we've found. It would be *so* exciting if it was there. When do you think we should do it, Isabella?"

"Not now," replied Isabella firmly. "Wait until everyone gets accustomed to the idea. Maybe tomorrow?"

Laura's face lit up. "So you are staying!" She turned to Leon. "Can you come back tomorrow?"

"I guess so." Leon looked up. "But I should go now. Grandma will be waiting."

Laura knew this wasn't true but she didn't argue. "We'll go out the front door," she said. That way he would not have to face everyone again. The sounds of shouting and laughter from the kitchen were getting louder.

"See you tomorrow, Leon," called Isabella. "Don't be put off by us. We may be a little wild, but Laura is right; we don't bite." She winked again at Laura. "And you thought I didn't hear!"

Laura was relieved to see Leon almost smile. Maybe it was just the suddenness of so many people arriving, she thought. People he didn't know. She understood how unnerving that could be.

The front door was stiff from lack of use; Laura had to wrench it open. From the doorstep, she had a clear view across the garden and noticed for the first time an indentation in the grass where the statue in the photograph must have stood. She turned to point it out to Leon but saw that he was staring vacantly at the weeds in the stone urn at the base of the steps, his lips pressed tightly together.

"Isabella is all right, really," she said, forgetting the statue. "She's just a bit startling at first. You will come tomorrow, won't you?"

Leon did not look at her. His gaze shifted to the gate. "What time?"

"I don't know. Ten o'clock, maybe? No, eleven. Then everyone is sure to be up."

"OK." There was a momentary pause. "See you then."

Laura watched him descend the steps and start along the path. He looked terribly lonely as he slipped through the gates and onto the road. The sounds from the kitchen drifted out to her but she felt somehow reluctant to go back in. When Samson wandered up, she sat down with him on the doorstep in the warm sun.

"What do you think about Leon?" she asked, running her hand over his fur. "What do you think has happened to him?"

Samson's only reply was to roll over and rub his head against her knee.

## ← CHAPTER 16 →

When eleven o'clock the next morning came, Leon was not there. Isabella had managed to persuade Laura's parents to let them take off one board — Hugo had looked and said that he could easily replace it. Laura had found the tools. Everything and everyone was ready, but Leon did not arrive.

Laura went out to the gate and looked down the empty road, trying to decide what to do. She'd had an uneasy feeling all along that he would not come.

After they had waited almost an hour, she jumped up. "I'll go and get him."

She grabbed her sweater, pulling it on as she left the kitchen, and, as soon as she was through the garden, started to run. Why had Leon said he would come if he didn't mean to? Just what was he so worried about?

She reached Mrs. Murphy's house and was about to fly through the gate when she caught sight of Leon. He was not alone. To her surprise, he was with the disheveled man she had seen in town on the long weekend, and they appeared to be in the middle of an argument.

It was not Harry and Isabella that had stopped him from coming, she realized—it was something else altogether, and she had stumbled right into the middle of it. It was too late to retreat. Both Leon and the man had turned to her.

"I can't come, Laura," Leon said sullenly. "You go on without me."

"Leon, what's all this about?" asked the man.

"Nothing." Leon now looked directly at Laura, a plea in his eyes. "Go on without me."

"We can wait," said Laura. She had not understood until that moment just how much she wanted him to be there when they pulled off the board. "Isabella and Harry aren't leaving until this afternoon. It won't be the same without you. We'll wait."

"No." Leon was adamant. "I'm not coming. You go ahead."

"Not going where?" asked the man, looking from Leon to Laura.

"Nowhere," said Leon. "It doesn't matter. Good-bye, Laura." His eyes were still fixed on her face, but the plea was stronger.

Laura backed away, recognizing the finality in his voice. He wasn't going anywhere. Not now, at any rate.

"Good-bye," she said, and started up the hill.

This time she did not run. Her feet dragged, her thoughts a mess. What was going on? The man must be Leon's father—he looked so much like him. But why were they arguing, and why was Leon so distressed? Laura picked up a stone and began tossing it from one hand to the other. How long had Leon's father been at Mrs. Murphy's? And why hadn't Leon said he was there?

When she arrived home, Isabella was sitting on the back step, sipping coffee. "So we scared him off completely, did we?"

"No, it wasn't you." Laura shook her head. "Not today, anyway." She sat down next to Isabella and began drawing in the gravel with a stick. She could still see Leon's father clearly in her mind. He didn't look like a criminal—not that she actually knew what a criminal looked like, but she was sure Mr. Murphy wasn't one. Something was definitely wrong, though. His clothes were so shabby and his skin was sallow and there were deep lines across his forehead. Just how long had it been since Leon's mother died?

Isabella put her arm around Laura's shoulder. "Shall we start without Leon?"

Laura hesitated. "No, we'll wait," she said. "He might come later."

But he didn't. The afternoon wore on and clouds moved across the sky, threatening rain. Harry, Isabella, and Hugo began talking about leaving before the storm started.

"If we're going to take a board off, honey, we'll have to do it now," said Isabella.

Laura chewed her fingernails and deliberated. "All right," she said. "We'll just see. There probably isn't anything there, anyway."

Isabella found Hugo and they headed for the hall. Laura followed, but somehow, without Leon, it didn't feel so exciting. In fact, it felt a little silly. Despite her father's concern, levering the board off proved quite simple and left little mess, but perhaps, Laura thought, it was just that Hugo knew what he was doing.

"OK, Laura," said Isabella when Hugo had finished, "where's your flashlight?"

Laura shone the weak beam into the darkness. There, falling away from her, was a flight of steps — and at the bottom, dimly visible in the wavering light, was a small room. It appeared to be empty but, when her eyes adjusted, Laura saw that there were shelves on one side with bottles lying on them. There was dust everywhere.

"You were right," shouted Isabella, peering over Laura's head. "There *is* something there."

"Should we take off some more boards?" asked Hugo.

Isabella's eyes were sparkling. "Of course!"

Hugo expertly levered off enough boards to make an opening big enough to squeeze through. "You go first," he said to Laura.

Gingerly, Laura stepped into the hole and felt her way down the steps, steadying herself against the rough wall. Isabella and Hugo followed close behind.

"It's just full of old bottles," said Laura when she reached the bottom. She shone the light on the bottles.

"Wine bottles," corrected Isabella.

"Very old wine bottles," said Hugo. He picked one up carefully, blowing the dust from the label. "Laura, you have found a treasure!"

Laura stared at the writing. It was in Italian, with a crest above it. The crest had leaves surrounding a plumed helmet and a serpent. She looked around.

The floor was brick and so were the walls. Everything was covered with dust, and there was a musty, faintly sickening smell pervading it all. Stale air in stale rooms. It was hard to feel excited about some dirty old bottles.

"So there is a cellar?" called her father.

"Yes," answered Isabella. "And what a cellar! It's full of wine. Come and see."

Soon the cellar was also full of people, and there was hardly room to move. Laura felt a need for fresh air. She climbed back out and sat on the floor in the entrance hall.

"I wonder what all this is worth," she could hear her mother saying from below. "We might be able to pay for some repairs with this. Look at this bottle. 1900. A good year, do you think?"

"Won't it all have gone bad?" called Laura from above. "It's awfully old."

"That makes it all the more valuable—if it is a good wine," said Harry, emerging from the cellar cradling a bottle in his large hands. "And this looks like it is very good wine."

"Of course it is." Laura rested her head against the wall. "It belonged to Mr. Visconti."

She wished that Leon was there. It did not seem

right to be finding all this without him. Her mind went back, as it had been doing all afternoon, to Mrs. Murphy's yard. Laura couldn't get the image of Leon's father out of her head. But it wasn't just his shabby clothes or his untidy haircut. It was his eyes, so like Leon's. Filled with surprise, but with something else, too. Concern? Pain? Worry? She suddenly thought that something inside him was crushed. Like his clothes—crushed and torn. She felt terribly sad, thinking of him.

As she watched Hugo and her father pull off more boards, and as Isabella and her mother talked excitedly, Laura thought how strangely everything had turned out. She and Leon were the ones who had started the search, but it was her parents and their friends who were now fired with enthusiasm, making lots of mess as they tore down the wall and speculated about Mr. Visconti and the house and its history. She just felt numb. Even when Harry, Isabella, and Hugo decided to stay on for two more days—to savor the celebration, as Isabella said—Laura did not feel elated.

Later, when all was quiet and the others were chatting and sipping wine (*not* Mr. Visconti's), she slipped back to the cellar and stood in the shadows thinking. She had brought the flashlight, but she did not use it—not at first. She just stood there, imagining an old man, immaculately dressed, with his hand on the wall, feeling his way down the steps, pausing in front of the bottles, drawing one out and carrying it back up to drink it alone in his garden room. When Laura switched on the flashlight, she almost expected to hear his accented voice quavering, "Who is there?"

The beam illuminated the shelves and the bottles through particles of dust. Laura shone it into the corners and onto the rough floor and walls, but there was nothing.

Nothing. *He's not here*, she thought. *Mr. Visconti has gone.*

She had an odd feeling that she wanted to cry. She felt as though she had lost something—something she never had. As she turned to leave, she caught sight of a dark shape under the bottom shelf. It was a metal box. She stooped to pick it up, then stopped.

No, she would wait.

She would wait for Leon.

## CHAPTER 17

Monday morning, for the first time, Laura hoped to meet Leon on the way to school. She was so desperate to tell him about the cellar, she didn't care who saw them together. He did not appear, however, when she passed Mrs. Murphy's house, and she did not see him as she crossed the school grounds.

They were halfway through their first class when he arrived. He handed a note to Miss Grisham and sat down without even looking at Laura. Laura stared at him, willing him to turn around, but he didn't. He just opened his book and started working. Perhaps he did not want to be seen talking to *her*. This was a new idea for Laura, and she was not sure how she felt about it. She returned to her work, trying to concentrate on the descriptive paragraphs Miss Grisham had asked them to write.

"I want you to make me see what you are describing," Miss Grisham said. "I want every noun to have an adjective."

Ever since the incident between her and Miss Grisham, Laura had refused to do any work in English. Or rather, she had refused to put any effort into her work. She did precisely what she was asked to do; no more, no less.

Today, however, perhaps because of all that had happened, when Laura started writing she found the words flowed onto the paper, and she was carried away on a wave of inspiration.

It was only afterward that she thought about the consequences and by then it was too late; Miss Grisham had asked her to read her paragraph aloud to the class. For one reckless moment Laura wondered whether she could just make something up, but realized that if Miss Grisham collected the papers afterward, she would be in more trouble. The class was staring at her expectantly, and she could hear the usual sniggering.

Laura opened her mouth and then closed it again. Taking a deep breath, she began dully, reading as fast as she could to finish as quickly as possible. "The air in the night garden was heavy with perfume. It drifted over the stone walls and leaked through the iron gates. The flowers, so vivid and colorful in the afternoon sun, were black now, soft shapes sprouting among black leaves. A black fountain sprayed black water over black figures. And, somewhere in this blackness, a voice was singing an aria, a sad and plaintive song. A song of lost hope. The music rose and fell like the breeze that rustled the black leaves. Then, suddenly, it stopped."

"That was very good, Laura," said Miss Grisham. "You might like to use some other adjectives instead of *black* to avoid repetition."

Laura groaned inwardly and sat down. If she had wanted to use other adjectives, she thought, she would have. But she had wanted to use black to emphasize the lack of color, the darkness, the secret nature of the sorrow—the sorrow she felt sure had been in the garden, her garden, along with the beauty and . . . something else that she sensed, like a perfume hanging over it.

When Miss Grisham asked Sally Jenkin to read her paragraph, Laura darted a glance at Leon. He was drawing something on the edge of his page, his hair falling over his eyes. Laura thought sadly how much he looked like his father.

At recess she took a long time gathering up her books, wondering if Leon would come up to her, but he didn't, so in the end, she went outside and stood near the door to the math room, waiting for the next class. She watched the other kids lounging around and joking with one another. They all seemed to find it so easy—why was it always so hard for her? Standing alone, she felt conspicuous, so she opened her book and began to read. She did not see Kylie, Maddy, and Janie approaching.

"That was a funny piece you wrote," sniggered Janie, stopping in front of her.

Laura jumped. Maddy rolled her eyes at Janie. "Yes, very . . . black."

"You could almost say *haunted*." Kylie leaned in close. Laura looked back at her book. Would they never leave her alone?

"Sophie Matheson said she saw you in the library with Leon Murphy," continued Kylie, giggling. "Are you hanging out with him now?"

Laura said nothing. Surely they would stop soon if she just ignored them. She tried to focus on the words in front of her.

"You should, you know," Kylie pushed, the tone in her voice turning darker. "You suit each other. You're both weird."

"Perhaps he's her boyfriend," scoffed Janie.

"He's not!" burst out Laura, tears filling her eyes as the girls all started laughing. She swallowed; if she began to cry, she would never live it down. Never.

Then, unexpectedly, she heard someone say, "I liked your piece in class, Laura."

She swiveled around to see Jenny Peters standing behind her. In the whole time Laura had been in high school, Jenny had never spoken to her. Girls like Jenny Peters did not speak to girls like Laura Horton. Jenny was the coolest girl in Year Eight. She had long blond hair and perfect skin, and her blue eyes sparkled. She was always picked first for sports teams. She never had to worry about wearing the right clothes or saying the right things. And she never had to stand on her own at recess, hoping someone would speak to her.

Laura mumbled, "Thanks." She didn't know what else to say. But as they all moved into class, out of the corner of her eye, she could see Kylie and Maddy staring at each other in astonishment.

Laura avoided Leon for the rest of the day. If people were talking about them like that, she was glad that he had not come up to speak to her. As she came out of their last class, she almost bumped into him but glanced away hastily and continued walking.

She had decided to open the box herself when she got home — she figured it would not matter, given that Leon was no longer interested. She tried to block out of her mind how much fun it had been searching for the cellar with him. After all, he hadn't even asked her what they had found. She collected her bag and headed for the gate.

The road ahead of her was empty except for a straggling quartet of Year Twelve students, who ignored her. She hurried along, her gaze on the ground, deliberately looking away from Mrs. Murphy's house as she passed it. If Leon wasn't interested, she didn't care. She was halfway up the hill when she heard someone running behind her. She turned sharply. It was Leon.

Clutching his side and gasping for air, he stammered, "So did . . . you find . . . anything?"

Laura opened her mouth, ready to tell him she never wanted to see him again, but as her eyes met his, her anger vanished. He was looking at her with the same mute appeal that had been on his face the previous day. Whatever reason he had for not coming over yesterday or meeting her this morning, it was not because he wasn't interested. Before she realized it, the words were out.

"We found the cellar."

"Oh."

Laura could hear the disappointment in the flatness of his voice. He really *had* wanted to be there. "There were bottles of wine in it. Very old bottles of wine."

For a moment she thought Leon was not going to respond. He kicked a tuft of grass, looking away from her. "Was that all?" he asked.

"No." Laura paused. "There was a box."

Leon scuffed the grass again. "What was in it?"

"I don't know."

Leon looked up. "You don't know?" he said incredulously.

"I was waiting for you," replied Laura. Then she smiled at him. "I haven't told anyone about it. It's hidden under the bottom shelf."

"Is it locked?"

"I don't know. It's a metal box. Come and see." She seized his arm and started pulling him up the hill. Leon laughed, and when she looked back at him, she saw that his eyes were bright with excitement.

She forgot what Kylie and Janie had been saying; she forgot about school completely. She was just glad to have Leon back again.

The heavy iron gates were pushed open, and Harry's car was still parked in the driveway. Leon glanced at it, then his gaze shifted to the garden and he grinned at Laura.

"I liked your paragraph," he said. "Miss Grisham doesn't know what she's talking about."

Laura flushed. "I was thinking of Mr. Visconti."

"I know."

Everyone was sitting around the table when they entered the kitchen. Hugo's voice boomed out over the general laughter, and Laura's father was holding a coffeepot in the air. Laura dumped her bag in the corner and waved hello.

"We're still here," Isabella called to Leon. "Has Laura told you about our discovery?"

Leon nodded.

"I've made a cake," said Harry. "It's a special, only-to-be-eaten-after-school cake."

"We'll be back," Laura assured him, and headed for the door to the hall, Leon close behind.

The gaping hole under the stairs was dark. Laura picked up the flashlight and led Leon down the uneven steps. At the bottom, she shone the beam into the corner where she had glimpsed the box. It glinted in the light. Leon whistled and squatted down to look at it more carefully.

"Well?" asked Laura, trying to keep her excitement contained. "What do you think?"

"Interesting," replied Leon. "Shine the light at an angle, and I'll try to get it out."

The box was wedged under the shelf, and at first they could not move it. Finally, with Laura pushing the shelf up and Leon pulling, they managed to drag it out. In the light, they could see that the lid had a design etched upon it. Laura brushed the dirt off and, running her finger over the pattern, said, "I think it's silver."

"It doesn't look like silver," objected Leon. "It's not shiny."

"That's because it's tarnished."

Leon shook it. "There's something inside. Listen."

Laura could hear it, too: the soft thud of something falling when Leon turned the box over.

"Open it," she urged.

"I can't. It's locked."

"Are you sure?"

"You try."

Laura grasped the lid and tried to maneuver it up. It would not budge. She dug her fingernails into the join, but still the lid would not lift.

Then she stopped, her eyes meeting Leon's. "The key!" she exclaimed. "Let's try the key!"

## ↞ CHAPTER 18 ↠

When they returned to the kitchen after retrieving the key from Laura's room, Harry was spreading whipped cream over the first layer of his cake. "It's a hazelnut torte," he said. "A work of art, don't you think?" He added another huge scoop of whipped cream and started sprinkling raspberries on it.

"It looks fabulous, Harry, but we can't stop now," replied Laura. "We'll be back, though."

He looked curiously at the box in Laura's hand. "What's that you've found?"

"Just a box." Laura glanced at Leon and saw the corner of his mouth twist up.

They hurried on, down to the tree house in the old orchard. It was the first time that Leon had seen it.

"This is fantastic," he said as they scrambled up through the spreading branches. Laura realized that he was the first person she had taken up there since it had been finished.

"It's my aerie. It's where I come to write." She took a deep breath and reached into her pocket for the little box with the tiny key in it. "Do you think it's going to fit?"

"It's worth a try."

Her fingers fumbled a little, but she managed to slide the key into the lock. Then it stuck. She could not turn it, and she could not pull it out. Frustrated, she shook it a little.

"Careful, Laura. It might break. Let me have a try." Leon closed his eyes and began to jiggle it. After a moment they heard a tiny click.

"It's open," he gasped. "It *was* the right key!" They stared at each other. "Of course the box may not have anything to do with Mr. Visconti," he added.

"It will probably just be full of boring papers," agreed Laura. "Like receipts for the wine."

"Or bills."

They both looked at each other again.

"Just hurry up and open it," implored Laura.

Leon lifted the lid. Inside there was a small package wrapped in brown paper with a faded blue ribbon tied around it. "Here," he said, handing the parcel to Laura. "You should be the one to open it."

Laura tried to untie the ribbon, but it fell to pieces

in her hands. Gently, she folded back the brittle paper and there, gazing up at her from a faded photograph, was the face of a young woman. Her eyes were bright and intelligent. They seemed to be laughing, although her lips were demure and her stance — hand on a chair against a backdrop of velvet and ferns — was very sedate. Dark curls escaped from their combs and fell over her high forehead. Looking at her, Laura thought that she would like to have known her. She turned the photograph over and written in elegant copperplate across the back were the words: *With my love, Veronica.*

"Veronica," she whispered. "Her name was Veronica."

There were other photographs underneath, all of the same woman. Veronica sidesaddle on a horse, her back straight, her dress falling in soft folds over the horse's flank. Veronica standing beside a flight of steps in a garden. Veronica looking out over a lake. And then, at the bottom of the pile, Veronica with an exquisitely dressed young man, who was leaning on a stick. Leon picked up the photograph and turned it over. The photographer's details were on the back but there was no writing.

"Firenze," he read. "That looks a bit like Florence. I think the photograph was taken in Florence."

Laura gazed at the two figures. She tried to imagine Mr. Visconti and Veronica walking through Florence, arm in arm, laughing. Or maybe strolling through a museum or gallery. They looked so young and so happy. As though everything was in front of them. What could have happened? She started turning over the other photographs, reading the photographers' details, but they were all written in Italian. There were no other messages.

"I wish there was more," Laura said. "I wish there had been more in the box."

"At least it wasn't full of old bills." Leon grinned at her. "And now we know what Veronica looked like."

Laura bit her lip. "I wonder how the box ended up in the cellar."

Leon frowned. "There's something funny about it. It's too shallow." He lifted it up and shook it carefully, but nothing moved.

"It probably just has a thick base," replied Laura, turning back to the photographs.

"No." Leon was still frowning. He turned the box upside down and examined the joints. Then he tapped on the sides and felt the edges, but nothing happened.

Laura grew impatient. "There's nothing there.

Let's go and show the photos to the others and have some cake."

Leon gave the box one last shake, then put the pictures back in it and followed Laura down the rickety ladder. Everyone was still in the kitchen when they returned, laughing, arguing, and drinking coffee. Harry immediately cut large slices of the cake and passed them to Laura and Leon.

"For our discoverers," he said. "Try this. It's my best cake yet. I am giving up sculpture. Cooking is my art from now on!"

"Bravo," called out Isabella, brandishing a fork.

"We've discovered something else," said Laura, taking the plate. She looked around at everyone proudly. "We've discovered some pictures of the person Mr. Visconti was in love with. The person he built this house for. Her name was Veronica."

She took the photographs out of the box, and everybody leaned forward to see. Laura smiled at Leon, happy that he seemed a little more comfortable today. At least he was not backing away toward the door. He was sitting at the table with his cake in front of him, watching everyone's reactions.

"What an interesting face," reflected Laura's mother, picking up one of the photographs to examine it more closely. "I wonder what happened to her in the end."

"Mr. Visconti must have loved her very much to build this house." Isabella shook her head sadly. "I hope she didn't just break his heart."

"Of course she didn't." Laura was indignant. "Something happened. And we're going to find out what." She took back the photographs.

"Isn't it amazing that the box has been hidden in the house all this time and no one knew?" said Laura's mother. "It's a good thing you forced us to look behind those boards, Laura. What did you think of the cellar, Leon?"

Leon had just taken a mouthful of cake. He swallowed quickly, almost choking. "It's dark."

"If it weren't for Leon, we wouldn't have found the cellar at all," said Laura's father. "I think he deserves a share of the wine."

Leon shook his head and was about to say something when Laura jumped in.

"Yes, he does. It was because of him that we started looking for the cellar in the first place. And I would never have continued if he hadn't insisted on going on." She grinned at him.

"The wine may not be worth anything, of course,"

warned Laura's father. "Don't set your hopes too high."

"It will be worth a lot," said Hugo firmly. "It is good wine."

"Of course it is. It's a lost treasure." Isabella was about to burst into song when Harry interjected.

"I've got an idea," he said. "You must stay for dinner, Leon, and we will celebrate the cellar. I'm cooking a special recipe. It will be wonderful."

Laura turned to Leon. "Yes," she said, "you must stay, Leon. Harry will be mortally offended if you don't."

"And we didn't have a proper celebration last night because you weren't here," added Isabella.

"I'm sorry, I-I-I can't," stammered Leon, flushing. "My dad is staying at Grandma's."

"Ask him, too," said Laura's mother. "And your grandma, if she'd like to come."

Laura waited for Leon to refuse. She saw him hesitate and then, to her amazement, he said, "Grandma wouldn't come. She never goes anywhere."

"Well, ask her anyway. Why don't the two of you go down now?"

Laura could not believe her ears when Leon agreed.

They took the box into Laura's bedroom and left it on the chair under the watchful eye of Samson, who was curled up on the bed. "Guard it well," said Laura, and Samson blinked in reply. Then they headed off down the road. Leon had gone silent again, and Laura wondered whether she should warn him that the meal might be a bit strange. In the end, however, she decided not to. After all, he had met Harry and Isabella; he could probably imagine what the evening would be like.

Leon's father was sitting on the veranda, reading, when they reached Mrs. Murphy's house. He looked up at the sound of the gate opening and took off his glasses, swinging them between his fingers as he watched them approach. Now that Laura had time to study him, she could see the similarities very clearly. The same high cheekbones, the same dark eyes, the same measuring expression. But she could see the differences, too. This man had none of Leon's defiance. Behind his measured gaze he looked utterly defeated.

"You must be Laura," he said, his voice low and curiously husky. "I am glad that we are going to meet properly this time."

Laura felt suddenly tongue-tied and simply nodded.

"Laura's mom has asked us to dinner," said Leon, sitting down on the veranda steps. "They have some friends visiting and one of them is cooking a special meal."

"Won't we be in the way?" asked Leon's father.

Laura found her tongue again. "Oh, no," she said. "Harry loves to cook for lots of people. He would really like you to come. He says he needs an audience; cooking is his art."

Leon's father looked questioningly at his son, then smiled at Laura. "I should be honored. What time do you want us to arrive?"

"Harry's meals are always late," Laura replied, trying to calculate how long it would take Harry to prepare his feast. "We probably won't start until eight thirty, but you can come any time you like."

"What about eight o'clock, then?"

"That would be good. I'll let everyone know."

"They asked Grandma, too," said Leon, "but I said she wouldn't want to come."

"No," agreed his father. "She probably won't. But you should ask her anyway. She'd like that."

Leon disappeared inside, and Laura stood on the path, waiting. She looked down at her shoes, struggling to think of something appropriate to say. But nothing seemed quite right. She shifted from one foot to the other.

"Leon tells me that you're a writer," said Mr. Murphy, smiling at her again.

Laura could feel her cheeks turn a bright red. "I just write stories. Sometimes . . ." Her voice trailed away.

"He says you're very good."

Laura looked back down at her shoes. How could she reply to that? But, somewhere deep inside her, she felt warm because Leon thought she wrote well. What else had he told his father?

"Leon is very good at math," continued Mr. Murphy after a pause. "Did you know that?"

Laura nodded. "Yes."

"He's been offered a scholarship. A wonderful scholarship, but he doesn't want to take it."

Laura looked up, her eyes wide. She realized then that she did not want Leon to go away.

Leon's father was looking at her gently, sadly. "Maybe you could talk to him."

At that moment Leon came back onto the veranda. He eyed them suspiciously but did not ask about the conversation. "Grandma would rather stay here but she says thank you very much." He swung himself up onto the veranda balustrade and wrapped his arm around the post. "She says she would come out but she's making marmalade and doesn't want it to burn."

"Did you tell her about the photos?" asked Laura.

"No. She was too busy."

Leon's father raised an eyebrow. "What photos?"

"We found some photos in the cellar," said Leon. "Photos of the woman Mr. Visconti built Laura's house for."

"Ah, more clues for your mystery. Like your postcard." He smiled and turned to Laura. "Leon has been telling me all about your house. I'm looking forward to seeing it. It's very beautiful, I remember."

It dawned on Laura that Leon's father must have grown up in this town — grown up in this house, in fact. Of course he would know of Mr. Visconti's house.

"Have you ever been inside it?" she asked curiously.

Leon's father shook his head. "We never moved in those kinds of circles. I used to ride my bike past it, though. A family lived in it then, but the children were away at boarding school and I seldom saw them. They went to the Grammar School," he added with a sidelong glance at Leon.

"Did people talk about the house much?" asked Leon.

"No, it was just the big house on the hill that the rich people lived in."

"We're not rich," said Laura quickly.

Leon's father smiled at her. "That was just our perception. Maybe the Harrisons weren't all that rich either. I don't think that they were at the end, anyway. The property became very run down."

"It still is," said Laura.

"It's very beautiful, though," added Leon.

His father smiled at him. "I'm sure it is. Leon tells me your mom is a sculptor, Laura. She must enjoy having all that space."

"Yes." Laura was surprised that Mr. Murphy understood so much about making things. Most people didn't realize how much room was needed or how much mess was made. She wanted to ask him what he did, but something held her back; if he had a job, surely Leon would be living with him.

"And now you've found some more space," he said. "Was there anything else in the cellar?"

"Just some old wine." Leon's voice was suddenly tense. He slid off the rail. "You'd better tell your mom and Harry that we're coming, Laura. We'll see you later."

Laura wondered why he did not want to talk about

the wine but could see the "off limits" sign in his eyes again, so she said, "All right. See you, Leon. Good-bye, Mr. Murphy."

"Call me Colin," said Leon's father. "We'll see you at eight o'clock."

Laura nodded and set off back up the hill. So Leon had been offered a scholarship. She frowned at the sidewalk. Why would he not want to take it? And why would his father suppose that she could make him change his mind? What could she say to convince him? And did she want to try? Laura shook her head and continued walking. She did not want to think about it anymore.

When she arrived home, Isabella was decorating the table for the dinner. She had arranged an enormous pile of oranges and red onions in the middle and was strewing ivy around them. The candles had been brought out again and distributed around the room. As she worked, Isabella sang, her voice drifting out into the dusk. "What do you think?" she called as Laura entered the room. "Will your boyfriend like it?"

"He's *not* my boyfriend," Laura said hotly, blushing furiously. "He's just . . . someone at my school."

"*O mia amore*," sang Isabella, draping ivy around

Laura's head like a wreath and laughing at her. From the way she sang it, Laura was glad the words were not in English.

"What is Harry cooking?" she asked, to change the subject.

"Roast beef and mushroom pie." Isabella adjusted one of the onions, almost bringing the pile crashing down. "And a pear tart. And little cheese things to nibble. When is your friend — who is a boy and is not your boyfriend — coming?"

"Eight o'clock. I'm going to see how Harry is doing," Laura called as she escaped to the kitchen. Harry, she thought, would be less interested in Leon.

But he, too, was full of questions. "What does your friend like to eat?"

"I don't know."

"He's not a vegetarian, is he?" Harry looked up anxiously from the slab of meat he was cutting, knife poised in the air.

"I don't think so. No, he isn't. He would have said if he was." At least, she hoped so.

Harry breathed a sigh of relief and went back to chopping the beef. "His grandmother grows vegetables, you said?"

Laura, who had been leaning against the table,

straightened up. Why did everyone want to talk about Leon all of a sudden? "Yes," she said, grabbing a carrot stick and heading for her room.

There she sat, cross-legged on her bed, thinking about everything that had happened—about Mr. Visconti and Veronica, about Leon and his father. So many unanswered questions, so many tantalizing mysteries, all intertwined in her mind. She reached for the box and opened it. There was the face of Veronica, gazing up at her. Laura ran her fingers over the photograph, as though trying to touch the woman who looked so steadily back at her.

"Why did you not come to this house?" she whispered. "What happened?"

## ❧ CHAPTER 19 ❧

It was dark by the time Leon and his father arrived. Isabella had lit the candles, and their light shone softly through the long windows, glinting on the dark foliage of the rosebushes and illuminating the large white magnolia flowers that had opened after the last brief shower of rain. Leon's father paused in the garden to breathe in the perfumed air. He looked, Laura thought as she watched from the ballroom window, like a poet in his best clothes. Leon, too, had changed and slicked down his hair. He was rather awkwardly holding a bunch of flowers — marigolds from Mrs. Murphy's garden.

Laura felt shy, as though she did not know this transformed Leon. She waited until her mother had answered their knock before she came into the kitchen. When she did, her mother was holding the marigolds and Leon, looking embarrassed, was staring at the floor.

"Some wine, Colin?" Harry asked Leon's father. "Red or white?"

"I'll just have something soft," he replied, glancing toward Leon. "I don't drink anymore."

Laura caught Leon's quick intake of breath and saw the muscles around his mouth tighten. What was it about the wine? No one else noticed, though, and the grown-ups continued moving around the kitchen, getting drinks, offering seats, and doing the things that grown-ups do. Laura and Leon stood on the edges, watching.

Laura heard her father ask Colin what he did and saw Leon's father hesitate. "I've been out of work for a while," he replied. "I used to do drafting."

"We're always out of work," said Isabella cheerfully. "Or out of the work we want to do. Let's drink to the solidarity of the workless."

Over the clinking of glasses, Laura's mother asked, "You've heard about the kids' discovery?"

"A little." Leon's father smiled his gentle smile.

"It looks as though they may have found a treasure. Hugo says the wine in the cellar could be worth thousands of dollars."

Leon's eyes grew wide.

"But they're just dirty old bottles!" exclaimed

Laura. "How could dirty old bottles be so valuable?"

"They may be dirty and they are certainly old," said Hugo, "but what is in them will turn out to be very exciting. I am ready to wager a bet on that."

"I wonder why the cellar was boarded up," mused Laura's father.

"This house is full of such mysteries." Laura's mother poured herself another glass of wine. "It is part of its charm."

Laura was about to say it would not lose its charm if they could solve its mysteries when Harry let out an exclamation and rushed to the oven; he had remembered his mushroom pie. After a lot of commotion in the kitchen, he produced it to great applause and they all followed him as he carried it triumphantly into the dining room. Laura saw Colin's eyes light up when he glimpsed the table, transformed by candlelight and the wild, luxuriant swaths of ivy.

Leon did not speak much during the meal, but neither did Laura. They both piled their plates with Harry's delicious concoctions and watched the adults laughing, talking, passing food, and lifting glasses. Laura was relieved to find that Leon's awkwardness appeared to have vanished. He was almost relaxed, sitting back in his chair, his fingers playing with a strand of ivy. His eyes were often on his father; Laura noticed how pleased he seemed that his father was joining in the conversation. At one point Colin and Isabella even discovered they had a mutual friend, a musician who was scraping out a living making coffee in a city café. Soon they were all talking about people they knew and what they were doing.

Laura nudged Leon, and they slipped away from the table. She led him to the ballroom, past the lumps of metal and stone, twisted and contorted in the dim light, to her corner at the end where the old sofa was pushed against the wall. They sat at opposite ends of the sofa, Laura curled up with her legs beneath her, Leon sprawled against the cushions.

"Your dad said you won a scholarship," began Laura almost accusingly.

Leon scowled. "It's because of the math. Because of that competition. You know those two days I was away? That was when I went for the interview. Dad thinks I should take it, but I don't want to. What would I do at some stuck-up private school?"

Laura started to say, "Nothing," but then stopped, changing her mind. She had remembered the expression on his father's face when he had asked her to talk to Leon. "Maybe you could just try it," she suggested. "You wouldn't have to stay if you didn't like it."

"Is that what you would do?"

Laura laced her fingers together, avoiding his gaze. "I don't know. But you're braver than me."

"No, I'm not."

"Yes, you are." She stopped twisting her fingers and looked across at him. "You moved to this town, for instance."

"That wasn't brave. I had no choice. I couldn't stay with Dad."

"Why not?" The words were out before Laura had time to think about them. She held her breath, wondering how Leon would react.

For a moment she was sure he was going to clam up. She saw his jaw clench, and he stared down at the floor. But, slowly, he began speaking. "Dad wasn't coping too well then. After Mom died. He was drinking too much. That's why he lost his job and everything."

Laura thought back to the day Leon arrived at the high school and how miserable he had looked. What must it have been like to lose his mother and then watch his father breaking down? She felt a lump in her throat.

"We didn't have any money or anywhere to live so

I came to stay with Grandma while Dad was trying to sort himself out." Leon looked up at Laura. "If you tell anyone about this, I'll never speak to you again."

"Of course I won't!"

"It's all over now. He's not drinking anymore and he'll have a job soon—he's got some interviews. He's clever, you know, really clever. He could have done anything, only Grandma didn't have the money for him to continue studying."

It was all suddenly clear to Laura. "That's why he wants you to take the scholarship," she said. She looked at Leon tentatively. "I think it would really help him if you took it."

Leon fiddled with a tassel on one of the cushions. "I'd have to board at the school," he said. "I'd hate that."

"You could come back here during the holidays."

"My dad will have a home then. I would go there."

Laura felt desolate but she heard herself saying, "And there will probably be kids like you there, kids interested in math."

Leon stared at a piece of driftwood propped against the wall. "I suppose I could try it," he said. "I know it would make Dad really happy."

"When would you go?"

"Next year."

*Next year.* Laura had a horrible feeling that she was going to cry. "It'll be fine," she said, jumping up. "Let's go and get some dessert."

Leon followed her out into the hall, his eyes puzzled. They could hear the laughter coming from the dining room and see the candlelight flickering on the walls. The smell of freshly brewed coffee and warm, sweet pastries drifted out to them.

As they reached the doorway, Leon caught Laura's arm. "If I did go," he said, "would you write to me?"

"Sure," replied Laura.

Leon brushed her hair lightly with his fingers. "It looks good."

"What?" Laura put up her hand. The ivy wreath was still caught in her hair. Blushing, she pulled it out. "I'd forgotten it was there," she said. "It was just Isabella playing silly games."

She turned to go, the ivy trailing from her hand, but Leon was still gripping her elbow. He hesitated before letting go, then said, "I've had a great time tonight. Thanks." Without waiting for a response, he slipped past her into the room.

"Just in time," Laura heard Hugo boom. "We've cut the pear and almond croustade."

## CHAPTER 20

When Laura saw Leon ahead of her the following afternoon, she quickened her step. "I brought the photos to show your grandmother," she said as soon as she caught up to him. "I thought she'd like to see them."

"She would," replied Leon, then added, "Dad said your parents insisted on giving him two bottles of the wine. They're going to sell them and give us the money."

"I know. We wouldn't have found them if it hadn't been for you. You were the one who read about the cellar. And you insisted we keep looking for it. I would have given up."

"It was both of us who found the cellar." Leon kicked a stone into the gutter. "Maybe something good will come from wine for a change." He paused, then looked away from Laura. "Dad had to go back to the city this morning. Just before he left, I told him I'd go to that school."

"Oh." Laura felt her stomach lurch. She swallowed and, trying to keep her voice steady, said, "So you'll be leaving at the end of the year."

Leon nodded. "You can't tell anyone, though. I don't want everyone knowing."

"Of course not."

They were both silent as they walked up the path to Mrs. Murphy's house. Even though the sun was shining, Laura felt as though a cloud had descended over everything.

In the kitchen, Mrs. Murphy was sitting in a large armchair. She had a shawl wrapped around her shoulders and her feet were raised on a low footstool. The television in the corner was switched on but she looked as though she had been dozing. "My rheumatism's bad today," she said, shifting uncomfortably in her seat. "Maybe some proper rain is coming at last."

Leon dropped a light hand onto her shoulder. "Laura has brought some photos to show you, Grandma," he said. "The photos we found."

Her face lit up. "That's lovely of you, dear," she said, smiling at Laura. "Fancy you finding them in the cellar like that. Leon, make us a cup of tea, will you, and then we'll look at them. There's some fruitcake in the tin. And you can switch that television off. It's all rubbish anyway."

Leon put the kettle on the stove and took a large tin out of the cupboard under the window. "Grandma's fruitcake is very good," he said, lifting the cake onto a plate.

"And so it should be," agreed Mrs. Murphy, "I've been making it for most of my life." She winked at Laura. "It would be a bad thing if I hadn't got it pretty near to perfect after all that time. My mother used to make these cakes to send to the soldiers during the war, to give them a bit of nourishment."

Laura bit into the thick slice that Leon had cut and thought about the soldiers who would have received the cakes. Such a strange idea, sending cake through the mail. But the soldiers must have been very grateful, because the cake was delicious. She hoped Mrs. Murphy would give her the recipe someday.

When they had all finished, Mrs. Murphy nodded toward the photos. "I'll need my glasses," she said. "They're on the table in the sun-room, Leon. Laura, pass me that tray, please. All right, I think I'm ready."

She went through each photograph, pausing for a long time when she came to the one with Mr. Visconti. Watching her, Laura had a fleeting image of

Mrs. Murphy as a little girl, running after Mr. Visconti down the dusty street. She looked at Leon, wondering if he was imagining the same thing. But Leon was watching her, an odd expression on his face.

At last Mrs. Murphy spoke. "What a handsome man. I can only just recall his face. Of course he was so very much older when we used to see him." She sighed. "How happy they look together—how young and full of hope."

Laura smiled. She had thought exactly the same thing.

Mrs. Murphy put the photograph down and shook her head. "It's terrible the way things go wrong between people," she said. "Well, thank you for bringing them over. I think you should show them to Janet, too. I'm sure she would like to see the pictures of her relative."

Laura thought of the sharp, unwelcoming woman who had peered at her through the wire screen. She was not so sure; Miss McInnes hadn't shown any interest in her own family history. She looked across at Leon for an answer.

"I guess we could take them around but she may not let us in," he said to his grandmother. "She was very unfriendly to Laura."

"She'll let you in." Mrs. Murphy's eyes glinted. "I'll tell her to."

After another slice of cake, Laura followed Leon out through the dark hallway to his small bedroom just behind the hall curtain. She had imagined that it would be like the other rooms in the house, cluttered with an assortment of furniture, but this room had only a bed, a chair, a chest of drawers, and a large wooden bookcase that was full of books.

"This was my father's room," said Leon, dropping onto the bed. "Those are his books, most of them."

Laura ran her hand along them, reading the spines. There was *The Jungle Book*, *Just So Stories*, *Biggles*, and a lot of books about chess and mathematics. At the end were some poetry books. "I can picture your father reading these."

"So can I," agreed Leon. "I like being in his room."

Laura could see that. He looked completely relaxed. She remembered how she had shivered when she had looked down the hallway, thinking how awful it would be to have to stay with Mrs. Murphy. How wrong she had been.

She sat down on the chair. "I don't want to visit Miss McInnes again. I wish we didn't have to show her the photos."

"But don't you see?" replied Leon. "If we show her the photos, she might give us some more information. She might be more willing to help." Then he grinned at her. "And anyway, she may not be so unfriendly after Grandma has spoken to her."

"Maybe not," admitted Laura. She looked down at the little bundle of photographs in her lap. She felt very protective of them. "OK," she said reluctantly. "I guess we could go after school tomorrow."

## CHAPTER 21

It was much less intimidating walking up Miss McInnes's tidy garden path with Leon beside her, Laura decided. They rang the egg-timer doorbell and waited.

When Miss McInnes appeared, she still seemed rather tense, but at least this time she opened the wire screen. "Rosie said that you had something to show me."

It took Laura a moment to realize that she was speaking about Mrs. Murphy. "Yes," she replied. "It's something that belonged to Mr. Visconti."

Miss McInnes eyed the plastic bag Laura had wrapped the photos in and said, "Well, bring it down to the kitchen."

It was the neatest kitchen Laura had ever seen — and the cleanest. Miss McInnes took an ironed tea towel from a drawer, spread it on the gray laminate table in the middle of the room, and indicated that

Laura could put the parcel on it. Laura felt a sudden rise of desperation. How could she show Miss McInnes the photos? She was so cold and unsympathetic. She would never understand.

"We found these in the cellar at Laura's house," Leon said when Laura remained silent. "They are photos of Mr. Visconti and someone named Veronica. Grandma said that you are distantly related to her."

Miss McInnes did not confirm this, but her eyes were watchful as Leon took the photos out of the bag. When she saw how many there were, she said ungraciously, "You had better pull up some chairs."

Laura and Leon sat on the edges of the cold vinyl seats and Leon handed Miss McInnes the photos while Laura smoldered about Miss McInnes's lack of warmth. Her house seemed to magnify sounds, and Laura became intensely aware of the ticking of the clock on the wall and the humming of the fridge in the corner. She glanced sideways at Leon and rolled her eyes; Leon grinned back at her. Miss McInnes studied the photos closely, then put down her glasses without saying a word.

After an awkward silence, Leon spoke. "We wondered if you might have any other photos of Veronica or Mr. Visconti. Or know anything else about the story or where we could look for more information."

Miss McInnes shook her head. "No, I told Rosie all I knew. Veronica's mother was my father's cousin. I never met her, and the whole story was only talked about in whispers. Mr. Visconti was a foreigner, after all—a most unsuitable suitor."

A most unsuitable suitor! Laura glared at the marblelike swirls in the tabletop and ground her teeth as the clock continued to tick in the background. She stole another glance at Leon. He was watching Miss McInnes calmly with his considering expression.

"I don't know any more about it," continued Miss McInnes after a pause, "but I did hear that Veronica died and that her father was a broken man after that. He had no other children, so I suppose he had nothing else to live for. The house and land just went to rack and ruin."

"What was her last name?" asked Leon.

"Mackenzie. Her father was Lachlan Mackenzie."

"And what happened to the property?"

"It was sold and subdivided into smaller farms The house is still there. It has been turned into a bed-and-breakfast, I believe. It still has the old name—Kirriemuir."

Laura saw Leon stiffen. "Was there a family graveyard?" he asked.

"I wouldn't know. There may have been. I don't think I can tell you any more."

Laura started gathering up the photographs. She couldn't wait to get out of there. A sense that she had somehow betrayed Mr. Visconti engulfed her; they should never have come. It was all she could do to mutter good-bye politely as they left.

Once they were out of earshot, she exploded. "She didn't even say thank you, Leon. You would think that she would have been interested in the photos of Veronica. It's her family history, after all."

"I think she was," replied Leon. "She just didn't know what to say. And you saw her house. She wouldn't know what to think about someone like Mr. Visconti."

Laura glared at the sidewalk. Deep down, she knew he was right.

"And she did give us some more information," he added. "You have to admit that. Do you think your mom or dad would drive us over to see that bed-and-breakfast place?"

Laura stopped abruptly. Her frown disappeared, and she gave a little skip of excitement. "I'm sure they would. We should see if Harry and Isabella can come too, and Hugo, if he is still in Melbourne. And your dad. We can all go on a picnic. Everyone who has been part of the discovery. What do you think?"

"I think it's a great idea," said Leon. He hesitated, then added, "Thanks for thinking of Dad. He really liked it with your parents." He paused again, looking away from Laura. "He still finds it hard to go out and meet people. I mean it's much better now but..." He thrust his hands in his pockets. "Anyway, thanks."

He looked suddenly very vulnerable. Laura was about to say that her parents liked his father too, hoping that it would not sound too trite, when Leon took his hands out of his pockets and said, "Come on. I'll race you to that tree."

Maybe she didn't need to say anything, she thought as she ran. He probably already knew.

# ← CHAPTER 22 →

Harry, Isabella, and Hugo drove up on Friday evening. The next morning Harry and Laura rose early to prepare the picnic. It was still dark outside, and even Samson looked sleepy as he sauntered in to demand breakfast. Laura was wearing three sweaters over her pajamas, and Harry had his parka zipped all the way up to his chin.

"We'll bake rolls," he said, rubbing his hands together to warm them. "I have a special Swiss recipe that you'll love. I'll show you how to make little echidnas with the dough."

Laura laughed. "Don't be silly. You can't make echidnas with dough."

"Yes, you can. Just wait and see."

While the dough was rising, they made cheese puffs and washed all the fruit and the vegetables. Laura found some baskets and started packing tablecloths, napkins, plates, and glasses. Then they rolled out the dough and made it into balls.

"Watch this," said Harry. With the air of a magician, he whipped a pair of scissors from his pocket and started cutting little nicks in the tops of the balls. Small triangles of dough stood up on end, just like prickles. "Now, bring me some raisins," he said. "And I need an egg, too."

As Laura looked on, he squeezed the end of the dough balls to make snouts and pressed the raisins in for eyes.

"There," said Harry. "Whip an egg yolk, and we will coat them with it to make them shiny. They have to look their very best for the picnic."

By the time everyone else got up, the kitchen was warm and smelling deliciously of freshly baked bread. On the table were lines of shiny little echidnas with bright black eyes.

"The only problem is—we will never be able to eat them," said Laura, dancing up and down with excitement.

"Don't you believe it," replied her father, and Laura had to hang on to his arm to stop him from biting into one right away.

As soon as Leon and his father arrived (Colin had caught the train up that morning), they piled into two cars and set off, just as the mist was clearing and the warmth of the sun was seeping through. Laura and Leon rode in the back of Harry's car, and Laura enjoyed watching Leon's surprise when Harry switched on the ignition and they began to rise. As they turned onto the main street, busy with Saturday morning shoppers, Laura caught sight of Maddy coming out of the café. Maddy's mouth dropped open as she watched them drive past. Laura looked away quickly, but to her astonishment, she realized that she was not particularly worried. That old feeling of terror about what everyone was thinking had gone.

"What shall we listen to?" asked Isabella, rolling down the window.

"Something Italian," said Laura.

Isabella found a tape of Vivaldi, and they drove with the music streaming out into the sunshine. The house was only fifteen miles from town, so it did not take them long to reach the turnoff to Kirriemuir Bed-and-Breakfast. They drove through cast-iron gates hinged to weathered stone pillars and down a long, dusty driveway lined with tall pines. The trees hid the house from view until they came over a rise. Then ahead of them they saw a cream rendered-brick homestead surrounded by a wide veranda. Laura and Leon both leaned forward in their seats, Laura trying to imagine what it must have looked like when Veronica lived there.

Laura was disappointed. "I thought it would have been bigger."

"I'm sure it was considered big when it was built," said Harry. "And impressive. Look at the stained-glass panels in the door and the pillars with the urns beside the steps. Let's get out and investigate."

Laura's mother had telephoned in advance to ask if they could visit, so the owners, Mr. and Mrs. Barlow, were expecting them. Mrs. Barlow came out to say hello, and while the grown-ups stood talking, Laura and Leon climbed the three low steps to the veranda.

"I don't think we are going to find anything here," whispered Laura. "It feels like everything has been swept away."

"You're always such a pessimist." Leon grinned at her. "You didn't think we would find the cellar either. Anyway, it's interesting just to see the house where Veronica lived."

The inside had been renovated many times. Mrs. Barlow said that they had bought the house three years ago. She knew nothing of the history, other than that it had been built by the Mackenzie family and that it had been sold when old Mr. Mackenzie had died in 1901. She had never heard of Mr. Visconti.

They all lingered in the narrow hall while she proudly showed them the newly furnished guest bedrooms, and then they went out to the airy sitting room for morning tea. Laura asked if it would be all right if she and Leon explored the garden while the adults were talking, and Mrs. Barlow smiled and nodded. They escaped through the back door and out onto the terrace. It was then that Laura saw it.

"Look." She grabbed Leon's arm and pointed. "The statue."

At the back of the neat knot garden, with its small box hedges and lacy cast-iron chairs, was a white, latticed arch. Standing beneath the arch was the figure of a woman holding a book. Leon looked perplexed. "What about it?"

"That statue was in *our* garden. Don't you remember? It was in one of the photos at the library."

"Are you sure?"

"Yes. Of course I'm sure." Laura started running toward it. "How on earth do you think it got here?"

"Maybe Mr. Visconti gave it to Veronica," Leon suggested.

They stood in front of it, looking up at the graceful figure, then Laura clapped her hands to her mouth. "Look at the face," she said. "It *is* Veronica."

"I think you're right," agreed Leon, moving so that he could study the face more carefully.

"I'm sure I'm right. And look at the book she's holding. It's a music book. Perhaps she was a singer. Maybe Isabella was right when she said that the house was made to be full of music. Mr. Visconti made the garden room for her to sing in"—Laura looked at Leon, her eyes wide—"and she never came."

Leon brushed away a cobweb clinging to the folds of Veronica's dress. "Perhaps she wasn't able to come," he said quietly.

They looked back up at the stone face gazing blindly across the neat garden to the blue sky beyond.

"Do you think one of Mr. Visconti's friends made the statue for him?" asked Laura.

"Possibly. Maybe Mrs. Barlow will know something about it."

"I doubt it. She doesn't seem to know much." Laura pursed her lips.

"It's worth asking, anyway."

Mrs. Barlow looked a little embarrassed when

they returned, bursting with the excitement of their discovery. "It was in the cemetery," she said after a moment's hesitation. "It wasn't on a grave or anything like that, so we didn't think that it would be a problem to move it. It was so pretty. It seemed to be wasted among the graves."

"Where is the cemetery?" asked Laura and Leon together. "Can we see it?" Laura held her breath, watching Mrs. Barlow. Her thoughts were flying in all directions. Why was the statue in the cemetery? It must have something to do with Mr. Visconti and Veronica. She felt a little shiver of fear—what would they find there? She wanted to know, and yet . . .

"It's in an enclosure by the back road." Mrs. Barlow began stacking the teacups. "It's just a small, private cemetery. There are only a few graves. I'll get Stan to take you down."

"You *were* clever to recognize the statue, Laura," said Isabella as they walked over the dry grass to the border of the property. "Don't you think so, Leon?"

Leon looked across at Laura. "I've always thought she was clever," he said.

Laura blushed. She wished Isabella wouldn't say things like that, but she was glad that Leon thought she was clever. Eventually, they reached the dam, which was almost empty, and the adults stopped to discuss the drought. Laura fidgeted in frustration. How could they be distracted at a time like this?

Leon nudged her and jerked his head toward the remains of a cast-iron fence. "Let's go," he whispered, and they set off, running down the slope.

Most of the fence had collapsed and lay rusting on the ground, grass sprouting through it. There were about thirty graves, all overgrown and weathered, some with broken headstones. Laura and Leon scrambled over the remains of the fence and began brushing aside the dry grass to see what was left of the inscriptions. There were a number of children's graves, and tears pricked Laura's eyes as she read them. Life seemed so fragile here in this forgotten corner. She looked up, dazzled by the sun, to find Leon standing on the other side of the enclosure. He was looking down at a curved headstone partly covered in yellow lichen.

"Here it is," he said in a low, unfamiliar voice. "Veronica's grave."

Laura's heart started pounding and her throat constricted. For a moment she couldn't move. Then, swallowing hard, she began walking toward him. Leon had squatted down and was clearing the grass around the headstone. It was weathered but the letters had been deeply carved and were still legible. *Veronica May Mackenzie. Born 1873. Died 1896. Always remembered.*

Laura's eyes blurred, and her heart felt as though it had turned over inside her. In a very small voice she whispered, "She was only twenty-three."

Leon nodded, not looking at her. He finished clearing the grass and stood up, dusting the earth from his hands. Laura swallowed again. The lump in her throat felt enormous. "Why did she die? What happened?"

Leon shook his head.

Despite the heat, Laura felt a chill run through her. She began to trace the letters with her finger.

"If she had lived today, it would probably never have happened, whatever it was," she said softly.

Leon did not reply. Maybe he had not heard. He was staring at a plain marble headstone a little farther away. "Look at that grave," he said, pointing. "It's newer than the rest."

Laura felt her heart turn over again. "Do you think . . . ? Is it . . . ?"

"There's only one way to find out."

They crossed to it and there, on the headstone, was the familiar crest. Below it was the other name they had been searching for: *Carlo Visconti. 1863–1938.* Under that was what looked like a poem:

> *Gentil pensero che parla di vui,*
> *sen vene a dimorar meco sovente,*
> *e ragiona d'amor sì dolcemente,*
> *che face consentir lo core in lui.*

Laura hardly dared to breathe. "So he *was* buried here, near Veronica," she whispered.

They both stood looking down at the grave, until the voices of the adults approaching broke through the stillness.

"What have you found?" Isabella called. "Are the graves there?"

Neither of them answered. Laura couldn't comprehend how Isabella could sound so cheerful, so unconcerned, when they had found something so momentous and sad. It seemed wrong that everyday life just continued on. When her mother put her arm around her and held her close, Laura snuggled in, thinking how glad she was that she had a mother who understood.

"What does it say?" Leon asked his father.

Colin did not respond immediately. Then he read the words in Italian, his voice catching a little. Laura thought they sounded like music.

"It's a passage from Dante," he explained. "Dante was a very famous Italian poet. Here he is speaking of his great love, Beatrice. He says: 'A gentle thought that speaks of you often comes to live with me and reasons about love so sweetly that it makes the heart agree with it.'"

"Oh, that's beautiful," sighed Laura. She was not exactly sure what it meant, but the sound of the words made her want to cry.

Leon's father nodded. "Yes," he agreed. "It is very beautiful."

"Was that where the statue was?" asked Laura's father, indicating a small stone pedestal set into the ground.

Mr. Barlow nodded. "We didn't know it was anything special," he said. "We just thought it would look pretty in the garden."

From under her mother's arm, Laura glared at him. "It was looking after Mr. Visconti's grave."

"You should take some photos," said her mother, giving her a squeeze. "It's a good thing we remembered the camera."

While the others sat on a nearby log, chatting, Laura and Leon took pictures of the graves and then wandered around photographing the surroundings. There was an unpaved road running past the cemetery but there were no houses in sight, and Laura was struck by how lonely and isolated it was. Like the story of Mr. Visconti and Veronica, it was being buried in time, buried and forgotten. She felt a tremor of anxiety. Was it right to be uncovering it again? It was a troubling thing, this exploration of the past. She looked at Leon. He had lowered the camera and was just staring out across the graves, as though thinking the same thing.

"How come your father can speak Italian so well?" she asked him later as they were walking back up to the house.

For a moment Leon said nothing. He looked at the brown paddock where the grass was stirring in a light breeze. Finally, he spoke. "My mother was Italian. Well, half-Italian. She was teaching him."

Laura felt as though all the air had gone out of her. "I'm sorry, I'm so sorry . . ." she stammered. "I didn't know."

"Of course not. How could you?" Leon gave her a twisted smile.

"This must be awful for you and your father."

Leon shook his head. "No, it's not. We're enjoying it. It's not our story; it's a different story. My parents did get married, and they were happy." He picked a stalk of grass and began to shred it. "That's why it's been so hard for Dad. When things are really good, it hurts all the more when you lose them, he says." He paused and then added, "When Mom was alive, Dad was completely different. He used to laugh all the time. And he had such dreams."

Laura looked at him uncertainly. "What happened?" she asked.

"It was a car accident. The other driver ran a red light." Leon tossed the grass away. "Come on," he said. "We should take some photos of the house and of the statue as well."

Later, when they stopped for their picnic in a nearby town, Laura saw Leon's father standing alone by a field, watching a cricket match being played on the dry oval. His shoulders were hunched, and he looked achingly sad. Leon had said that it was not their story, but, looking at Colin leaning against the rail, Laura could not help but think of Mr. Visconti.

They had both had dreams, and they had both lost them. A lump caught in her throat. She started to turn away, afraid that if she were to say anything, it would be the wrong thing. Then she saw Colin brush his hand across his eyes. Hadn't Leon said that his father found it difficult to be with people? She realized she was just being cowardly. She took a deep breath and walked toward Colin and, amazingly, she did know what to say, after all.

"Thank you for translating the poem."

He turned, and the sadness slipped from his eyes. "Thank *you* for letting me be part of the discovery," he replied, smiling. "You and Leon are uncovering a very beautiful story, I think." After a pause, he said, "And thank you for talking to Leon about the scholarship. I really appreciate it. It will be a good thing for him."

Laura was wondering how to respond when Harry called out, "Lunch is ready."

"Come and see our rolls," she said. "Harry and I made them this morning."

Together, they walked back to where the blankets had been spread out under a tall pine tree. Laura reached for the basket and, with a dramatic gesture, swept the cover off to reveal the nest of echidnas beneath.

Across the checked tablecloth, she smiled at Leon.

## ← CHAPTER 23 →

When Laura arrived at school on Monday, she was bracing herself for Maddy's attack. She fully expected her to have told Kylie and Janie about the outing with Leon in the crazy shark car. She had even planned how she was going to react when they started needling her.

To her surprise, however, no one said anything. When Maddy passed her in the corridor, she looked at Laura rather oddly but continued on. Later in the day Kylie, Maddy, and Janie actually smiled at her as they stood outside the math classroom with a group of students, discussing the end-of-the-year dance.

"I heard Ms. Lee say that it's going to have a sixties theme," said Maddy. "If it does, what will you wear?"

"I dunno. Beads and things, I guess," replied Janie. "What about you?"

"Same."

"My mom's got this long skirt with sparkles on it." Janie spun in a circle, as though the skirt was swirling around her. "Maybe I'll wear that."

"I hope it does have a sixties theme," said Maddy. "It would be really cool."

"I'd rather have a supernatural theme." Kylie flicked back her long hair and pouted. "Angels and devils. Something like that. Or pirates. I could do a great pirate costume."

"Are you going to come, Laura?" asked Jenny Peters, who was standing nearby.

Everyone turned to look at Laura. "I don't know," she replied. This was not strictly true. She had no intention of going.

Nevertheless, during class she found herself thinking about the dance like everyone else and wondered what it would be like. She imagined arriving in a beautiful dress, with her hair swept up and her arms swathed in bracelets, everyone turning to look at her and whispering as she passed by, "Doesn't Laura Horton look amazing?"

But that wouldn't happen, of course. She would not wear the right thing, and she would not have anyone to talk to. She would just end up standing in the corner, on her own, being miserable and wishing she had never come. She bit her lip hard. Why did they have to have a school dance? It would all be so much easier if they could just do their tests and finish the year without all the end-of-the-year activities—the sports days, the outings, and the dance. Particularly the dance, she thought crossly, biting her lip even harder.

Leon was waiting for her outside the gate after school. Glancing at him as they set off down the hill, she wondered what he thought about the dance. Probably nothing; he never worried about that sort of thing.

He caught her expression. "What?"

Blushing slightly, Laura replied, "Nothing. Have you started your history assignment?"

The rest of the way home, they talked about schoolwork, and when they reached his house, she went in with him to say hello to Mrs. Murphy.

"Ah," Mrs. Murphy greeted her, looking up from

the bowl she was stirring. "I hoped you'd stop by. Janet has been trying to get in touch with you. She wants you to call her. Here's her number." She wiped her hands on her apron and reached for a torn piece of paper with some figures scrawled on it.

Laura took it gingerly, trying to imagine what it would be like speaking to Miss McInnes on the phone. It was difficult enough face-to-face.

"Why does she want to talk to Laura, Grandma?" asked Leon, leaning over the bowl.

"She didn't say. She just said she'd remembered something and wanted to tell Laura." Mrs. Murphy rapped Leon's knuckles lightly with the end of her spoon. "Keep your fingers out. There are some cookies in the tin."

"Yes, but they're not as nice as these. When will they be ready?"

"In half an hour."

Leon turned to Laura. "Do you want to stay and have some when they come out of the oven? They're really good. You could call Miss McInnes from here."

Laura cringed at the thought of calling Miss McInnes, either here or at home. Still, she was anxious to know what Miss McInnes had remembered, so they went into the sun-room and, while Leon watched, she dialed the number Mrs. Murphy had given her.

"Hello?" Miss McInnes sounded even more irritable on the phone than in person.

"This is Laura Horton. Mrs. Murphy said you wanted me to call you."

"Yes." There was a pause. "After you left, I recalled a box of old family papers I'd put away in the cupboard. I've found a letter that may be of interest to you and the boy. If you'd like to come over tomorrow after school, I'll show it to you."

Laura's heart started racing. "That would be great, Miss McInnes. Thank you, thank you so much. We'll come at four o'clock."

Leon mouthed, "What is it?"

She mouthed back, "Wait."

"Mind you, don't be late, then. Good-bye." Miss McInnes hung up before Laura could reply.

"What did she say?" demanded Leon as soon as she put the receiver down. "Has she got something?"

"She's got a letter, and she says she'll show it to us! She wants us to come over tomorrow after school."

"Wow!" Leon let out a long low whistle. "I wonder what's in it."

"She didn't say. She just said she'd found it with some family papers. I bet she knew about it all the time."

"Maybe. It doesn't matter, though. The important thing is that she is going to show it to us. I told you she might be able to help us."

"I wouldn't call it helping, exactly."

Leon raised his eyebrows at her. "Yes, it is. You just don't want to admit it."

Laura crushed up the piece of paper with the phone number on it and threw it at him.

"Do you two want to lick the bowl?" called Mrs. Murphy from the kitchen. "I've just put the cookies in the oven."

It was hot in the kitchen, so they took the bowl to the back step and sat there running their fingers around the white plastic basin and talking about the letter and what it might contain.

Suddenly, Laura stopped licking her fingers and looked at Leon. "Thanks," she said.

Leon stopped licking his fingers, too, and looked back at her questioningly. "For what?"

"For helping to find Mr. Visconti. I would never have discovered all this by myself."

Leon grinned. "That's some admission, Laura Horton."

A little later Mrs. Murphy brought them a plate of warm cookies and two glasses of lemonade. A freight train rumbled by and, in the background, Mrs. Murphy's chickens clucked contentedly. Laura lifted her face to the sun. She was happy. School, the dance, Kylie, Maddy, and Janie seemed a long way away.

## CHAPTER 24

All the next day Laura could think of nothing but the letter. As soon as the last bell rang, she grabbed her books, dashed to her locker, and then ran out into the afternoon sun. Leon was already waiting for her at the gate and they set off, hardly aware of the curious glances of the other students following them through the main gates. There was no shade, and Laura could feel little rivulets of sweat running down her back under her schoolbag. *It's funny how quickly summer comes*, she thought. *Two weeks ago, it was still quite cool.*

Miss McInnes's neat little house was familiar to them now, and the egg-timer doorbell sounded less alarming.

Leon wiped the sweat from his forehead with the back of his arm and whispered, "I hope she offers us something to drink."

"I wouldn't count on that." Laura dumped her bag on the ground. The back of her dress was plastered to her skin. "She never offers us anything."

"Yes, she does. She's offering us the letter." ·

At that moment Miss McInnes opened the door, making them both jump. She unlatched the wire security screen and said, "Come in. Hurry. I don't want to let the heat in."

The hallway was oppressively hot, and they raised their eyebrows at each other behind her back, but the kitchen had an air conditioner on a portable stand and was blissfully cool.

"Put your bags over there," said Miss McInnes, indicating a space beside the back door, "and take a seat. Would you like a glass of juice?"

"Yes, thank you," they said in unison.

Miss McInnes took a glass jug from the fridge and put it on the table. The jug was covered with a white crocheted cloth weighted around the edges with blue beads, and Laura reached out to touch the beads, making them swing and tinkle against the glass. "This is very pretty," she said.

"My mother made it. People don't make things like that anymore, more's the pity." Miss McInnes looked across at them, as though they were directly responsible for the lack of needlecraft in the modern world. "They expect to buy everything."

Since there seemed to be no satisfactory reply to that, neither Laura nor Leon said anything. They sipped their drinks and waited. Miss McInnes went out of the room and returned with an old shoe box tied with a long brown shoelace.

"These are some papers my father kept," she said as she untied the lace. "They are mostly letters. There is only one that would be of interest to you. Here it is."

She handed Laura a thin envelope. In the left-hand corner was the crest they had seen on Mr. Visconti's grave. The stamps had *Italia* on them, and the address was written in flowing letters with a lot of flourishes. Laura looked at Leon for a moment, then slid the letter out and carefully opened it. The crest was on the paper, too. There was an address in the right-hand corner but, as it was written in Italian, it was hard to decipher. They could just make out the word *Milano* and beneath that the date, *14 settembre 1938*. The rest of the letter was in formal English.

> *Dear Mr. McInnes,*
> *I write with deep appreciation and gratitude*
> *to thank you for your letter informing me of*
> *the death of my cousin. It is many years now*

*since Carlo left his birthplace and his family to travel so far away to Australia, but I still hold his memory very dear. He was to me like a brother as we were boys together, and it saddened me greatly that we were not able to spend our adult years in closer contact. Carlo had the soul of an artist, and he looked always for beauty. When he met Miss Veronica Mackenzie, he believed that he had found it, and although he wrote to me to say that he was content, I think that he never recovered from her tragic loss.*

*After Miss Mackenzie died, he sent to me some sketches of the house that he had built for her. They are very delicate and show, indeed, the beautiful world that he wanted to create for her. I am an old man now and my years are not many. If you or your family would like the drawings, I will send them to you.*

*Accept, I beg of you, my most sincere regards,*
*Gabriele Visconti*


"Gabriele," breathed Laura. "*G*. It is the *G* from the postcard." She looked across at Miss McInnes, full of expectation. "Do you have the drawings?"

Miss McInnes shook her head. "I've never seen them. I don't believe that my father asked Mr. Visconti's cousin to send them."

Laura and Leon gaped at her in amazement.

"Why should he have?" continued Miss McInnes defensively. "We didn't know Mr. Visconti. My father only wrote to the family because someone had to inform them of his death, and there was no one else to do so. I believe that a representative came out to settle Mr. Visconti's affairs, but I know nothing of the drawings. After all, I was only a child at the time."

Laura's mouth was still dropped open. She could not believe what she was hearing. How could Miss McInnes be so uninterested in everything? So unfeeling? Did she not have *any* imagination?

"Would you mind if we copied the letter?" Leon asked, kicking Laura under the table. "Laura is keeping a record of everything that we've found. We could make a photocopy of it in the library and return it tomorrow, or, if you don't want us to take it away, we could just write down what it says."

Miss McInnes took her time to reply. "You can keep the letter if you like," she said. "I don't have any need for it, and it belongs with the house."

The reply was so unexpected that it was a moment before either of them could absorb it.

"Thank you, thank you so much," burst out Laura as soon as she found her voice. Without thinking, she jumped up and gave Miss McInnes a hug.

Miss McInnes turned red. "That's all right," she said brusquely, patting Laura awkwardly on the back. "Be careful with it."

"We will," they chorused.

They were still saying thank you as they backed out the door into the heat.

"I can't believe she gave us the letter," exclaimed Laura as soon as they were on the sidewalk. "I was just thinking what an unimaginative, boring, unsympathetic sort of person she was, and she *gave* us the letter."

"I know." Leon nodded. "I thought she had no idea what we were talking about, what we were trying to do." He turned to Laura. "You know what? I think we should write to the address on the letter. Maybe they still have the drawings. Maybe they would send us a copy of them."

Laura eyed him doubtfully. "The writer was an old man. He was the same age as Mr. Visconti. He would have died a very long time ago. There might not be anyone who has even heard of him at that address."

"On the other hand, there might be," said Leon. "It's worth a try."

Laura looked down at the envelope. "It will be like sending a message back in time." Her fingers ran over the row of stamps. "As though we are writing a letter to someone who no longer exists. About people who no longer exist." She paused for a moment, then added, "It's strange, though; they feel very real to me, all those people."

"And to me, too," replied Leon. He swung his bag around onto his other shoulder. "I think we should write the letter right away."

Laura nodded. "Yes. Come back to my place now. We'll write it together."

The coolness in Laura's kitchen was quite different from the coolness in Miss McInnes's kitchen. It was the coolness of thick walls and shady vines, of high ceilings and the insulation of rooms above. A coolness that you could sit in for a long time, thought Laura as she took a bottle of water from the fridge and found some clean glasses in the cupboard—something that was never an easy task. They both sank down onto chairs, and Laura took out the letter.

Suddenly, from the studio, came a series of loud bangs. Leon jumped but Laura hardly stirred. "It's just Mom," she said. "She must be moving things around."

A moment later her father appeared in the doorway, followed by Samson. "Do you think we have a resident giant now?" he asked, shaking his head. "If so, I shall have to talk to him about wearing slippers. He really does need to consider his fellow occupants."

Laura smiled. "I think he's just passing through."

"I'm glad to hear it!" He ran his fingers through his hair. "How are you, Leon?"

"I'm good, thank you," said Leon.

Laura wondered if Leon was ever going to stop being so polite and formal when her parents were around. She turned back to her father. "Dad, do you have any writing paper?"

"What sort of writing paper?"

"Good-quality writing paper. Very good quality. We want to write to Mr. Visconti's family in Italy."

"You'll need an address, you know. You can't just

write to the Visconti family, Milan. There are lots of people named Visconti living there. They're an old Milanese family."

"How do you know that?" asked Laura.

"I looked it up on the Internet."

"Oh." Laura looked at him. So her father had been doing some research, too. "Did you find anything about Mr. Visconti?"

Her father shook his head. "No, nothing. I would have told you if I had."

"Well, *we* have found something. We have found an address!" Laura sat back to let the magnitude of this sink in.

She was not disappointed. Her father raised his eyebrows and came over to the table to sit down. "All right then, I'm impressed," he said. "Really impressed. Tell me everything."

When she had finished, Laura said, "So now you see why we need very-good-quality writing paper."

Her father nodded. "I do indeed, and I think I have just the thing. Let me go and rummage."

While he was gone, Laura did a bit of rummaging herself and found some granola bars in the back of the pantry. "I think they're still all right."

"They look OK." Leon took one and peeled off

the paper. "I'll be the food tester this time," he said, grinning at her.

Laura smiled back. It seemed like a very long time since that first day when he had come to see the house. "There are some apples, too," she said, moving the bowl to the table. "I know *they're* all right."

When her father came back, he was carrying a gray box and some pens. "This is very fine paper," he explained, opening the box. "Your mother gave it to me because she liked the watermark." He held up a sheet to the light so that they could both see the delicate tracery of a rose in the creamy paper. "There are envelopes as well, and I have brought some good pens for you to try."

Laura threw her arms around his neck. "It's perfect," she exclaimed. "We'll figure out what we want to say and then copy it onto the paper. It will be just right."

"Well, I might go and see how the giant is getting on while you do that," said her father. "Have fun." He headed for the door.

Deciding what to say was not simple. It was late and all the granola bars had been consumed, along with several apples, before they were finally ready to copy what they had written onto the writing paper.

"You should do it," said Leon. "Your writing is better than mine."

Laura did not argue; she had seen his untidy scrawl. Carefully, she started to reproduce the words on the paper. Then she copied the address onto the envelope, hoping she was transcribing the Italian correctly and, after looking to Leon for reassurance, sealed the envelope and placed it on the table. "I'll mail it tomorrow."

## CHAPTER 25

Once they had sent off the letter, all they could do was wait.

The school term dragged on. Everywhere, posters for the dance were appearing, and it seemed to Laura that nobody was talking about anything else. She was having trouble concentrating, too—her thoughts were full of Mr. Visconti and Veronica. Every day she hurried home, hoping for a reply to her and Leon's letter.

The week before the dance, Laura was walking home with Leon, wondering whether today would be the day when the letter would come, when he stopped abruptly. "I want to ask you something."

"Yes?"

"I was wondering if you wanted go to the dance."

Laura stared at him. "What?"

"I mean, I was wondering if you wanted to go with me."

"I thought you didn't like things like that," she stammered. This was totally unexpected; not in a million years did she think Leon would ask her to the dance. She felt sick with anxiety. Whatever was she going to say?

"It's OK. You can say no if you want to."

"It's just I . . . I never go to dances." She felt as though the words were coming out all wrong but she couldn't stop herself. "I don't like them. I think they're silly."

"So that's a no, then," said Leon.

"It's not that I don't want to go with *you*. I just don't want to go." It was no use. She could see that he did not believe her.

He shrugged and turned away. "Whatever."

Laura watched him walk around the side of Mrs. Murphy's house. She felt terrible. It was true, she told herself; she didn't like dances. At least, she *wouldn't* like them if she went to them. Yet, somewhere deep inside her, she knew that was not the reason she had said no.

She had said no because, in the end, she would have been too embarrassed to go with Leon, and she felt very, very bad about that.

The next morning, she left early and waited for Leon outside Mrs. Murphy's. When he came out, she tried to explain again. "It's true, what I said. I don't like dancing. And I haven't got anything to wear."

"It doesn't matter." Leon hunched his shoulders and thrust his hands deep into his pockets. "I don't care."

"We could do something else."

"Just let it go."

Laura wished fervently that yesterday had never happened. Things had been going so well. Why did Leon have to spoil everything by asking her to the dance? They walked on in silence, neither looking at each other.

As they arrived at the school gate, Jenny Peters was unloading a pile of large plastic bags from a car. They were full of streamers and posters.

"Hey, Laura," she called out, "can you help me carry these? They're for the dance."

Laura turned to Leon, but he had already walked off without saying good-bye.

"Sure," she replied, hurrying over.

The bags were bulky and difficult to carry. They kept slipping from their hands and one dropped onto the ground, splitting open. A sudden gust of wind almost sent the reams of colored paper flying across the school grounds. Laura and Jenny bumped into each other trying to rescue them.

Jenny burst out laughing. "Quick, before another gust comes," she said, stuffing the streamers back into the bag and attempting to hold it closed.

"Yeah, otherwise we might end up decorating the school yard instead of the gym," said Laura.

"Imagine that!" Jenny's eyes met hers. Laura had a vivid image of the streamers swirling out over the school and began to laugh, too.

"Help, I think I'm losing my grip again," she said.

Jenny grabbed the bag just before it fell.

They struggled forward with their troublesome loads, giggling and calling instructions to each other, until they reached the hall. As they went through the door, Laura glimpsed Kylie and Maddy walking across the yard, staring at them.

"Thanks for that," said Jenny when they had

deposited the bags in the foyer. "I don't know what I would have done if you hadn't come along."

"I thought we were going to lose them," panted Laura. She felt light-headed, talking with Jenny Peters like this.

"Doesn't it look great?" Jenny waved her hand toward the gym, where a transformation was already taking place. There were large posters of the Beatles and the Rolling Stones on the walls as well as a huge psychedelic montage with rainbows and suns. A silver ball was hanging from the ceiling, catching the light on its mirrored surface, and three boys were maneuvering the sound system onto the stage.

Laura nodded. It did look wonderful. She had a sudden vision of the room full of students in swirling dresses swaying to the music under the dancing lights of the silver ball.

"You really must come," said Jenny. "It will be heaps of fun."

Laura thought of Leon. Why did everything have to be so complicated? Maybe it would have been fun to go to the dance, but it was impossible now — now that she had refused Leon.

She felt dazed all morning and hardly noticed

Kylie, Maddy, and Janie when she came out of the classroom at recess. They were standing by the door as though they had been waiting for her. To Laura's surprise, Janie offered her a chip and asked, "Have you decided to come to the dance, then?"

Laura shook her head.

"Why not?"

"I don't like dances."

She waited for a snub to follow, but instead it was Kylie who spoke. "Are you going away over Christmas?"

"No."

"Neither are we. It's not fair. We never go away. I'm gonna be stuck here all summer. Maybe I'll see you around."

Laura choked. "Maybe," she said.

"You want to go to the cafeteria? I'm going to get a doughnut." Kylie took out her wallet and smiled at Laura.

"No, I'm fine." Laura remembered the apple she was holding and polished it against her sleeve. "I'll see you in class."

As she watched the girls walk away, she chewed her apple meditatively. Was Kylie serious about wanting to hang around with her over the summer? What would they do? A little voice in the back of her mind kept saying that it would not be comfortable and fun like it was with Leon. She couldn't imagine Kylie wanting to explore an old house or talk about poetry or just sit on the veranda eating apples; she couldn't imagine Kylie wanting to do any of the things she liked to do.

She shook her head. No, she told herself, it *would* be fun. And anyway, Leon was not going to be there.

The following afternoon, Laura found herself coming out of the locker room after school at the same time as Kylie, Maddy, and three other girls. One of them was Jenny Peters.

"We're going down to Sam's Hamburger Joint. You want to come?" asked Kylie.

Laura almost fell over. What was happening? Her world had turned upside down since Jenny Peters had started talking to her. Now everyone was talking to her. Of course it was probably just because they wanted to be friends with Jenny—everyone wanted to be friends with Jenny Peters—but it was all very unsettling, and she was not sure how she felt about it. Ahead she could see Leon, lounging by the front gate, waiting for her. "No, I . . ."

"Come on." Jenny slid her arm through Laura's, steering her toward the other gate. "It'll be fun."

Laura saw Leon swing his bag over his shoulder and walk off. "OK," she said, trying not to think about Leon trudging home alone and feeling angry—or worse, hurt.

Laura had often looked at people sitting at the tables outside Sam's and wished she could do that sort of thing. She had thought it looked like so much fun. Now, unexpectedly, she found herself there, sipping a milk shake and watching everyone walk by. For the first time, Laura felt very cool and was enjoying being just like everyone else, doing something that everyone else did. She was glad that her mother had insisted she always have some emergency money—surely being asked to Sam's by Jenny Peters was an emergency. The milk shake, sweet with chocolate and rich with malt, tasted unbelievably good.

A group of older boys from another school was sprawled at a nearby table. One of them shouted,

"Whatcha doin' tonight? Want to come and join us?"

The girls all giggled. Despite feeling a little uncomfortable, Laura giggled, too.

"My mom said I can have spray tan for the dance," announced Maddy, still watching the boys from the corner of her eye.

Laura tried to imagine covering her body in fake tan and immediately pictured Leon's reaction; he would think it was ridiculous, she felt sure. She took another sip of her milk shake. What did it matter anymore, now that everything was ruined between her and Leon?

"You're so lucky. My mom says I'm too young. It's so unfair," said Janie.

"Did you hear that Susie is going to the dance with Michael Nguygen? He asked her last night." Maddy lifted her skirt a fraction to show off her long legs.

"Who are you going with, Jenny?" said Kylie. "Lots of boys must have asked you."

Jenny laughed. "No one." She licked the straw from her iced coffee. "Have you decided if you are going, Laura?"

Laura felt her face go red as everyone turned toward her.

"You could go with Leon Murphy," Maddy said with a giggle. "He's always walking to school with you."

Laura breathed in sharply. They couldn't possibly know he had asked her, could they? But as the girls began laughing, she realized with relief they weren't serious. She felt a rush of guilt, though, remembering what had happened. Leon really had wanted to go with her, and she had refused him. It hurt to think they were making fun of him.

"Laura's not going because she doesn't like dances," said Kylie. "She said so."

"Really?" asked Jenny.

Laura wound a curl of hair around her finger, desperately trying to think of what to say. Now that the girls were being friendly to her, perhaps she did want to go . . . but of course, that wasn't possible. Not now. "Yes," she replied, looking down into her drink.

"Why not?"

"She's too serious, aren't you, Laura?" said Maddy. "Not like us." She laughed a little tinkling laugh.

*Not like us.* There it was again. Laura heard the words drumming in her head. It was true, she thought. She wasn't like them. She didn't want to sit around at Sam's after all. She wanted to be at home in Mr. Visconti's house, curled up in the corner of her bedroom, doing the things she enjoyed. Sitting here at Sam's, all she could think of was Leon and whether he was still angry with her.

She stood up and reached for her bag. "I'd better be going."

"To your ghosts?" asked Maddy, laughing again.

"Yes," replied Laura. "To my ghosts." She looked directly at Maddy. "I like them."

Maddy stopped laughing and turned uncertainly to Kylie; Kylie was looking at Jenny, who was smiling at Laura.

"See you tomorrow," Jenny said. "Have fun with your ghosts." Somehow, the way she said it made the ghosts sound really cool.

"See you tomorrow." Laura shouldered her bag and set off down the street, wondering if Mr. Visconti and Veronica would mind being her ghosts.

Her thoughts kept going over everything that had happened. It was so confusing. All she had ever wanted was to be asked to Sam's with the girls. And now she couldn't wait to get home. Her pace quickened. Why had Jenny started talking to her like this? It was all very—what was that word her father used?—gratifying, but very strange, too. And how was she ever going to make things right with Leon?

She decided to stop by and apologize for not walking home with him. That would be a start. But by the time she was passing Mrs. Murphy's house, it was after five thirty. She knew they would be having dinner, so she continued on. She would talk to him tomorrow. Maybe her mind would be clearer in the morning.

Her mother was chopping vegetables for a salad when she arrived home. "I've hit a mental block," she said. "I've no idea where to go next, so I thought we'd have an early dinner. Have you and Leon been discovering more secrets?"

"No," replied Laura, feeling guilty, although she tried to tell herself she hadn't done anything wrong. "I was with some friends from school. We went down to Sam's."

Her mother looked up at her in surprise. "That's nice."

"Sort of," Laura mumbled, and headed for her room.

She threw her bag into the corner and plumped

down on her bed, disturbing Samson, who was asleep on the pillow. He gave a little mew of protest.

"Why can't everything be simple?" she murmured, picking him up and burying her face in his fur. "You don't have these problems, do you?"

Samson mewed again, telling her that he did indeed have problems; it was dinnertime, and he had not been fed.

## CHAPTER 26

Laura had to run to catch up to Leon the following morning. He hadn't waited for her even though she was sure he had seen her.

"I'm sorry about yesterday," she began, panting because she was out of breath.

Leon shrugged. "Why? You didn't do anything."

"I went off with Jenny and Kylie."

"That's your business." Leon continued to stare straight ahead. He had not looked at her.

"It was just that they asked me to Sam's. . . ." Laura could feel herself floundering.

"I don't care. It's fine."

"No, it's not fine." She grabbed him by the arm, forcing him to face her. "You're not talking to me."

"Yes, I am. What do you think I'm doing now?" His eyes met hers, but there was no smile in them. Laura was shocked to see that Leon had the same defiant expression he had had that first day at school.

She pressed her lips together. She wished she could feel angry about it, but she couldn't. She understood completely, and that made it so much worse.

"Why are you hanging around with those girls anyway?" he demanded. "They were so mean to you."

"They're not being mean now." Laura tried to forget Maddy's gibe about the ghosts.

"That's just because Jenny Peters has started talking to you. They'd talk to anyone Jenny talked to." He scowled at her. "And anyway, they're boring. They just giggle all the time."

"No, they don't."

Leon picked up a stick and threw it against a tree. He threw it so hard, the stick splintered in two. "If you hang around with them, you'll become like them," he said. "You'll become boring like them."

"I will not," said Laura furiously. "What's gotten into you, anyway?"

"Nothing. Nothing's gotten into me."

"That's not true," shouted Laura, and she stormed on ahead without him. If he was going to be like that, she didn't care.

She had other friends now.

As soon as Laura walked through the gate, Kylie jumped on her. "My mom said that Mrs. Sweet said that Leon Murphy's leaving. That he's got some sort of scholarship, and he's going to some private school. Is that true?"

"How would I know?" replied Laura, anxiety seeping through her. How did they know about the scholarship? A sudden dreadful thought struck her: what if Leon thought that *she* was responsible for telling them?

Kylie was watching her closely. "You're always with him."

"No, I'm not!" At least she wouldn't be anymore, not now that Leon wasn't talking to her, she thought with a pang.

"You need to be careful. If you hang around with nerds, you'll end up all nerdy yourself."

It was funny how they were both telling her that she should be careful who she hung around with. Then Laura reconsidered; it was not funny at all. It was awful.

Kylie tossed back her hair. "Anyway, I almost feel sorry for Leon. I bet he'll find it horrible at the new school. You know what he looks like. He can't even afford a proper haircut."

Laura squirmed. She felt as though she were betraying Leon. Why wouldn't Kylie stop talking about him? Why was she so interested in him, anyway?

Laura tried to edge away, but Kylie wouldn't stop. "And with his dad and all." She shook her head. "It'll be ghastly."

Desperate to escape, Laura spun around, only to see Leon standing behind them. For a moment his eyes met hers and she felt her stomach heave. Before she could say anything, he had pushed past her and entered the classroom.

All day, whenever she thought about it — and that was all the time — she felt sick. Waves of panic swept over her. As soon as school finished, she raced to the locker room, then ran after Leon.

"I wasn't talking about you," she blurted out as soon as she caught up with him. "It was Kylie. She'd heard about the scholarship. Not from me. From someone who knows her mother."

Leon said nothing.

"I wouldn't talk about you, Leon." He was walking

so fast, Laura struggled to keep up with him.

"It doesn't matter. I don't care." Leon did not take his eyes off the road ahead.

Laura tried to think of something else to say but couldn't, so they continued on in a painful silence, Laura still almost running, until they arrived at Mrs. Murphy's gate.

Leon went in without saying good-bye.

There were five more days until the dance. Five long, miserable days. Laura had never been so unhappy, not even when she had torn up her dragon. She did not see Leon when she walked past Mrs. Murphy's house, and he seemed to just vanish after school. He did not look at her in class either. Laura saw him on the other side of the room, working, reading, staring out the window, and she thought that her heart would break.

She missed him dreadfully. It didn't matter that Kylie, Maddy, and Janie talked to her all the time now or that Jenny Peters chose her to be part of her team for a basketball game. This was what Laura had been wanting, ever since she had started high school, ever since they had moved to this town.

But now that she had it, she didn't want it anymore. She just wanted to be friends with Leon again, to walk home with him and talk about Mr. Visconti and lick the cookie dough from the mixing bowl on Mrs. Murphy's back step.

On the day of the dance, excitement was buzzing through the school yard like electricity. The Year Eight classes were allowed to go home at lunchtime, and everyone spilled out into the sunshine, shouting and joking and jostling. Laura grabbed her bag and left immediately, feeling worse than ever.

For the first time since they had stopped talking, she saw Leon ahead of her. His shoulders were hunched, and he was walking very fast. Suddenly, she made a decision. She started to run, her heavy bag jolting against her back. When she caught up with him, he did not turn or say anything.

"Leon, stop," she said, grabbing his bag and

gasping for breath. "Stop. I want to ask you something." Leon stopped but he did not look at her.

Laura swallowed. "I was wondering if you still wanted to go to the dance," she said. "I was wondering if you wanted to go with me."

"Are you asking me to go with you now?" He was rigid, his gaze fixed on the train tracks.

"Yes."

There was silence.

"Why?"

"Because I want to go. I want to go with you," said Laura.

Leon looked at her then but his eyes gave nothing away. "So you've decided it's OK to be seen with me now?" he asked, although it was not really a question.

The words hit her like a blow. Laura shot him a reproachful glance and began running down the hill as fast as she could, her eyes blurred with tears.

"Hey," Leon called, sprinting after her. "Come back. I'd like to go with you."

Laura skidded to a halt. She turned back to him and her heart leaped. He was grinning his old grin.

"I'll come over at seven," he said, turning into Mrs. Murphy's garden. "See you then."

Laura crossed the tracks and started up the hill, feeling alive again. Everything was all right now. Leon wasn't angry with her anymore. They were friends again. He still wanted to take her to the dance.

Then she stopped, dropping her bag onto the road. But what was she going to wear? Laura began to panic. Everyone would look so good. They had makeup—not Isabella's theatrical makeup, but real, proper makeup—and they knew how to put it on. They had earrings and long dresses and swirling skirts. They had fancy shoes. They had fake tans.

Laura tried to think of anything in her wardrobe that would look even vaguely appropriate. But she had nothing. Nothing at all. She imagined arriving in her one good dress—it was too small now and looked like a little girl's dress. Everyone would laugh. The more she thought about it, the more desperate she felt. Catching sight of Samson asleep in the violet patch, she gathered him up for comfort and carried him inside. Her mother was making a sandwich in the kitchen.

"You're home early," she said, looking up in surprise.

"Remember, I told you. We got out at lunchtime today because of the dance."

"You don't look very happy about it."

Laura sat down, still clutching an indignant Samson. "I'm going with Leon."

"That's great."

Laura's eyes filled with tears. "But I've got nothing to wear. Everyone else will look so good and I'll just . . ." At this moment Samson, who had been struggling to get free, managed to jump onto the table. He leaped off quickly before he could be scolded and stalked out the door.

Laura's mother came over and gave her a hug. "It's all right," she said. "We'll work something out. What do people wear to dances?"

"I don't know," replied Laura in a small voice. "It's supposed to be a sixties theme."

"A sixties theme—why, that's easy!"

"What do you mean?"

"Wait and see." Laura ate half her mother's sandwich while she waited for her to return. When she did, she was carrying a red flowery dress with embroidery on the front and tiny sparkly mirrors stitched into it. "Try this on," she said. "Your godmother, Anna, gave it to me. She bought it when she was traveling in Afghanistan. Put it on."

They went into her parents' bedroom, the only room with a full-length mirror. Laura took off her uniform and slipped on the dress. It was a little too long, but her mother pinned up the hem.

"Wait a moment." She left and came back with some daisies to put in Laura's hair. "There," she said. "You look beautiful—like a real flower child! I'll sew up the hem, and you'll be fine."

Laura stared at her reflection. "Are you sure this is what people will wear?" she asked.

"Well, it *is* a sixties look. It's perfectly appropriate—and the important thing is, you look beautiful." Her mother kissed her.

Laura turned around, studying herself from all angles. She could not quite believe it. She did look beautiful. The white daisies were like stars in her dark curls, and the red dress made her cheeks glow. Her eyes were shining. Then she remembered her daydream about the dance. It was as though she had stepped into it and been transformed.

When Leon arrived at exactly seven o'clock, he was carrying a small bunch of roses. "Wow, you look fantastic," he said. Then, remembering the flowers, he thrust them at her. "Grandma said I should bring these."

But Laura did not see them. She just stood there staring at Leon. She hardly recognized him. His hair had been cut. He was wearing a new sweater, a college sweater for the sixties theme, and proper jeans.

Laura thought he looked amazing.

"My dad got that job I told you about," he said. "He sent me some money, to get ready for the new school. Do you think I'll pass?"

"Maybe." Laura grinned. "If you stop hanging around with me."

"Never," replied Leon, then added, "So are you going to take these flowers, or not?"

Laura laughed and took the bunch. "They're beautiful," she said. "I'll just put them in some water, and we can go."

## CHAPTER 27

Laura had walked the road to school over a hundred times but never like this. Never in a dress that swirled around her ankles and glinted in the soft evening light. Never with flowers in her hair and bangles on her wrists. And certainly never with someone who looked like Leon did now. She kept glancing at him shyly, wondering if he was quite real, and was reassured to see that he still had his measuring expression, that he still kicked a stone as he walked, and that he still scowled when he caught sight of Kylie, Maddy, and Janie hurrying through the gates ahead of them.

It was as though the same dreamlike magic had descended over the school, Laura thought. The old drabness was gone and there was color everywhere. In the girls' bright dresses. In the boys' shirts. In the streamers and balloons that billowed around the front of the hall. Even Mr. Parker looked colorful in an astonishing orange shirt. Only Miss Grisham remained the same; she stood at the entrance to the gymnasium, selling tickets and frowning at a group of boys hovering by the door.

Laura felt apprehensive as soon as she saw them. Were they going to start making fun of her? She steeled herself for their taunts, but none came. To her surprise the boys had become very quiet. Behind her, she heard someone calling. It was Jenny Peters.

"Hey, Laura, you look awesome! I'm so glad you came." She hugged Laura and then turned to Leon. "You look great, too, Leon. I barely recognized you." She grinned and nudged Laura. "So the rumors were true, after all."

There was nothing nasty in her tone, just friendliness, and Laura thought how strange it was that the same comment could sound so different, depending on who said it.

"What rumors?" asked Leon, looking from Jenny to Laura.

Before Laura had time to feel embarrassed, Jenny took her arm and said, "C'mon, let's go in."

As they entered the gymnasium, Laura found it impossible to believe that this magical place was where she had sat through endless assemblies and long boring speeches. Rainbows danced across the walls and ceiling as the mirror ball revolved and the psychedelic montage glowed under the spotlights. On the stage the sound system was a myriad of flickering lights, radiating music over the crowded floor.

"Look at our streamers," shouted Jenny above the music and the squeals of girls greeting one another. "They're free now."

Laura nodded, gazing up at the strips of silver and purple hanging from the ceiling.

"Come and join us, Jenny," yelled a girl in a bright pink miniskirt who had stopped dancing and was beckoning wildly from beneath the mirror ball.

"Catch you later. You two have a good time." Jenny let go of Laura's arm and began threading her way through the dancers. A moment later she was in the center of the room, moving to the music, her arms pumping the air.

Laura felt a wave of inadequacy sweep over her. "I could never do that," she said. "Let's just watch for a while."

Leon grinned at her. "Look at those girls over there. They're just moving from one foot to another. I'm sure you can manage that. And no one will notice you, anyway."

Laura was not so sure — Kylie was already staring

at her and whispering to Maddy and Janie—but she followed Leon onto the dance floor and began to shuffle in a small circle, trying not to think about how silly she must look.

Leon smiled at her. He appeared completely at ease. He stood quite still for a moment, listening to the rhythm, and then as though the music was running through him, his body began to move. Laura watched him, fascinated, until she realized that he was watching her. Then she stared up at the mirror ball.

After a while Laura forgot to worry about how she looked. She felt the music carrying her away. She sang snatches of the songs along with everyone else and, like them, called out for more when the music suddenly stopped and Mr. Bevan came to the front of the stage.

Mr. Bevan was acting as DJ, and although Laura did not have him for any of her classes, she knew that he was very popular. Under the lights, in jeans and a tight shirt, he looked much too young to be a teacher. He coughed into the microphone. "Now I've been told that some of you are going to dancing classes, so, even though tonight has a sixties theme, I think it would be good to put those dancing lessons to use.

How about something with a Latin flavor? A little salsa?"

There was an audible groan and people began to leave the floor. Laura pulled at Leon's arm. "I can't do that," she whispered. "Come on."

Leon didn't move. "You'll be fine. Just follow my lead."

"What?" Now there was panic in her voice. "No!" She turned away but Leon caught her around the waist, pulling her back.

He drew her close and whispered, "Back-step-step, forward-step-step."

Laura bit her lip and struggled to concentrate on the rhythm as they began moving slowly around the floor. She tripped over his feet several times and got tangled in her dress, but each time it happened, Leon steadied her and continued on. As the song drew to a close, he spun her around, catching her just as the music ended. She was still laughing when the music stopped. Everyone began to clap and Laura realized that they had all been watching.

Blushing, she said almost accusingly to Leon, "Where did you learn to do that?"

Leon raised his eyebrows but the music began again, and he did not reply.

"That was awesome," gushed Kylie, pushing her way through to them. "You were great. I wish I could dance like that." Kylie dragged her eyes away from Leon and glared at Laura. "I thought you said you didn't like dancing."

"Perhaps she didn't know she did," said Leon.

Laura wondered what was happening. Everything was changing. First Leon had appeared in his new clothes, then he turned out to be a good dancer, and now he was speaking to Kylie. Almost.

"I do like dancing after all," she said to Kylie. "Leon was right. I just didn't know it. Come on, Leon, let's go back."

After that Laura let herself enjoy everything—the transformed gymnasium, the music, the dancing. She wanted it to go on forever, but when the last song finally ended and they all spilled out into the warm night air, that was wonderful, too.

Jenny Peters and several of her friends walked part of the way home with Laura and Leon, laughing and joking. Laura liked that, but she liked it even more when it was just Leon and her, under the starry sky with the night sounds all around them.

"So how did you learn to dance like that?" she asked again after they had been silent for a while.

"My mother taught me. She used to dance around the kitchen to the music on the radio. If my father or I came in, she would grab us and make us dance with her." Leon's voice was warm with affection. "She knew all the steps. When she was dancing, it was like she became part of the music."

"She must have been lovely," whispered Laura.

"She was."

When they arrived at Laura's house, they didn't go straight inside. They sat on the front steps, looking out over the moonlit garden, and Laura thought she had never been so happy. She looked at Leon and wondered why she had ever worried about him and about school and about being different. She realized now that there was no one she wanted to be except Laura Horton who lived in the Visconti house and was friends with Leon Murphy.

She breathed in deeply. "You can still smell Mr. Visconti's roses."

"It's like in your paragraph," replied Leon. "The one Miss Grisham didn't understand. The air is heavy with perfume."

"Yes, it is, and the leaves and the flowers are velvety black." She brushed her hand over the camellia bush beside the steps. "Mr. Visconti seems very close here, doesn't he? As though he's still somewhere in the garden."

"Yes. As though he might suddenly appear, walking up the path or across the lawn. What would you do if he did?"

Laura thought for a while, then replied, "I would ask him what happened. What happened when he came out to Australia." They were both silent, imagining Mr. Visconti solemnly considering her question.

"You know . . ." Leon looked at her thoughtfully before continuing: "There's something about that box that has been bugging me. I've been thinking and thinking about it. It's way too shallow. I'm sure there's something in it we haven't found yet. Something else."

"What?"

"I don't know, but something."

"I'll go and get it," said Laura, jumping up. She felt certain that if they were going to find anything else, it would be tonight—tonight when everything was so wonderful.

Leon was talking to Samson when she came back. The cat had settled on the bottom step and was fastidiously licking his fur, his bell tinkling softly.

"Dad said I can have another dog once he gets settled," said Leon, scratching Samson. "I thought I would never be able to have another one, not after I had to give up Nero, but now, maybe . . ." He looked up at Laura. "Let's see the box."

Laura handed it to him. "I've brought a flashlight," she said, shining it onto the lid. "Maybe there's a secret keyhole."

Leon grinned at her. "It would hardly be secret if you could see it," he teased, and began examining all the joints and the intricate pattern on the top. Then he opened the box and inspected the inside. "Nothing," he said. "I must be imagining things."

"Let me look." Laura took the box and ran her hands over the outside. It was true. The base did seem very thick. She opened the lid and began to press against the fine silk lining. Unexpectedly, her fingers struck something hard beneath the fabric. Before she realized what had happened, one side of the box shot up, revealing a small drawer with a delicate clasp set into it.

Laura and Leon looked at each other, their eyes wide. "I told you so," said Leon. "What did you do?"

"Nothing." Laura was staring at the drawer in disbelief. "I didn't do anything."

"You must have done something. Go on. Open it."

Laura lifted the clasp and pulled. The drawer slid out easily, as though it was running on tiny tracks. In it lay a thin packet of letters. She gasped. "Do you think it is all right to read them?" she asked, her voice anxious.

She did not need to explain this anxiety to Leon; he, too, was looking at the letters with uncertainty. Carefully, he picked up the packet and turned it over. "I think it would be all right to read them respect-fully," he said at last.

Laura could not imagine any other boy she knew saying that. It was what made Leon different, she realized. Not the clothes or the haircut or the place he came from. It was the fact that he understood that they should read these letters respectfully. It was what, in the end, made her feel comfortable with him.

She watched as his long, capable fingers undid the ribbon around the letters—the same pale-blue ribbon that had been around the photographs—and slid the first one out of the envelope. Then she switched on the flashlight again. In the little circle of light, they began reading. The letter had been mailed in Australia to an address in Italy in 1893.

*My dearest Carlo,*

*We arrived home yesterday. The journey from Melbourne was hot and uncomfortable and Mama suffered greatly. She continues to feel poorly after the long sea journey. Everything is so dry here. So brown. So burned. I miss the green gardens and the soft skies. I miss the music and the Institute. But most of all I miss you. Sometimes I think that the pain is more than I can bear. I take out my locket and look at your face and the rosemary you gave me that evening in the Villa delle Rose, and it is like a knife twisting in my heart. Twisting pain and joy, like the locks of our hair wound around it. I count the weeks, the days, the hours until you come. Papa is still firm in his opposition. He frightens me sometimes with his obstinacy. And Mama is so frail that I do not like to trouble her with our problems. Sometimes I fear that they will never consent to our marriage. I need you close to give me strength.*

*With all my love,*

*Veronica*

Leon put down the letter and looked at Laura.

"Her father must have remained obstinate," said Laura. "That would be why she never came to live in the house, why they never got married."

"Maybe he didn't understand."

"Well, he should have. He was breaking her heart."

Leon opened the next letter. It was dated January, 1894.

*My dearest Carlo,*

*Why do you not write? I wait each day for your letter but it does not come. Have you not received my letters? Have you forgotten me so soon? I cannot believe that. I will not believe it. I am thinking of you now, wondering what you are doing. Are you in the library now at the Villa delle Rose? Is the fire lit against the cold? And is there a bowl of winter roses on the table by the French windows? Is the garden covered with frost? Here the sun continues to burn the landscape, and there have been fires. Not cozy fires in the fireplace. Terrifying fires, raging across the dry, parched earth. I had forgotten the heat. It is like a veil that hangs*

*over everything, distorting it, stifling it. It is impossible to escape. My throat is dry. I cannot sing. Maybe I will find my voice again when your letter comes.*
*Your loving,*
*Veronica*

"Why doesn't he write?" exclaimed Laura, her voice shaking a little.

"Maybe he does but she doesn't get his letters."

"That would be so cruel." Laura pictured Veronica standing in the hall at Kirriemuir, holding a pile of letters, none of them from Mr. Visconti, trying to restrain her tears. She opened the next letter and gently straightened out the crease.

*My dearest Carlo,*
*At last a letter! And such a letter! I have already read it a hundred times; it is wet with my tears. I can scarcely believe that you are really coming. After such a long time! You say that you have written before but I have not received your letters. I have heard nothing until this wonderful letter arrived this afternoon. I was in the hallway when the postman came.*

*Mary took the mail but I saw immediately that there was a letter from Italy on the top of the pile and asked for it. She seemed reluctant to give it to me, which was strange. She knows how anxiously I have been waiting. When I saw your familiar hand, I could hardly stop shaking. I took the letter to the conservatory and there, among the ferns, I opened it with trembling hands. After not hearing from you for so long, I feared that you were writing to say that you would not follow me. But no! Oh, Carlo, now that I know that you are coming, I can abide anything. Even the heat is not so insupportable. After I had read your letter and kissed the photograph you sent, I went to the piano and started to play. It was the first time I have done so willingly since I arrived home. And my voice has come back. I could sing again!*

*I live for the day when I will see you.*

*From your loving,*

*Veronica*


"I told you so," said Leon, his eyes lighting up. "He did write."

"And he did come." Laura wrinkled her forehead. "So why didn't they get married?" Then she turned to Leon, her heart filled with horror. "And what happened to all Mr. Visconti's letters? Her father must have taken them."

She reached for the next envelope, fumbling a little in her impatience to open it.

"This one is addressed to a hotel in Melbourne. The Windsor."

"What does it say?" Leon bent forward, his shoulder touching hers as they read.

> *My dearest Carlo,*
>
> *Papa remains obstinate. He refuses to listen when I try to plead our cause. And Mama grows weaker. Papa says that I must not trouble her and, indeed, I can see that he is right. She is too frail to spend more than two hours a day from her bed. He wants me to accept the hand of our neighbor, James Lambert. He tells me that it will give Mama peace to know that I am comfortably settled. How can he not understand that I could not be comfortably settled with anyone but you? Surely it would not bring peace to her to know that her daughter*

*is desperately unhappy. I am sending this letter early so that it will be waiting for you when you arrive. I long so much to see you but I am so frightened, too. Oh, what will Papa say when he discovers that you have come? How wonderful that you are coming!*

*As ever, with all my love,*

*Veronica*

There were only two more letters. Laura picked up the first one, shining the flashlight on the envelope.

"This is addressed to our house," she said. She looked up at the tall gray facade. "To Mr. Visconti's house."

"So is this one." Leon was fingering the other envelope. "And there is no stamp. It must have been hand-delivered."

"What does that mean?"

"I don't know." He put the letter back down. "Go on. Open yours."

They both huddled over the letter.

It was dated August 1895.

*My dearest Carlo,*

*People tell me of the house. Indeed, it is all the rage. No one speaks of anything else. How grand the ballroom is! How beautiful the murals! How elegant the gardens! My heart breaks with the pain of it. When we drive into town, which is such a rare event now, I crane my neck to glimpse the gray parapet rising above the rooftops. I imagine you there. Oh, my love, if only I could come to you. But Mama is so ill, and Papa is like a bear in a cage, growling at every little thing. It is so hard for me to get away. I live for the brief moments we spend together—but they are so painful, too. Sometimes I cannot bear it. When Mama is better, however, then we can be together forever. I long for that day.*

*My cough grows worse. I will send a message when I am better.*

*With my love—all of it,*

*Your Veronica*

Laura and Leon looked at each other, their eyes full of apprehension.

"I don't want to read the last one," said Laura, pushing it away. She did not want to know any more; it was too painful.

Silently, Leon slipped it from the envelope and unfolded it.

> *My dearest Carlo,*
>
> *It was more wonderful than words can tell to see you today — to see you here, in this house. I had thought that after that terrible, terrible day when you first came, you would never step back across this threshold. How dreadful it was when you stood in the hall, wet from the sudden fall of rain, and Papa shouted at you to leave. How dreadful when you stepped back out into the rain and walked slowly, so slowly, my love, down the long drive. And Papa slammed the door! But I must not think of that. Not now. I must not think of what might have been, only of what we have now. Dr Mitchell said that I was looking better after your visit, and I felt stronger. Perhaps tomorrow I will be able to sit in the drawing room. If only the cough did not leave me so weak. But I will get stronger now. I will get better. I pine already for your*

*next visit. Papa came to say good night, and*
*he was very sweet. He said that you were a*
*gentleman. As if I had not told him so, many,*
*many times. He looked so sad but he need not*
*be sad anymore. I will get better now that I*
*have you. I will even sing again.*
*Your loving,*
*Veronica*

Neither of them spoke after they finished reading. They did not look at each other. Laura switched off the flashlight and sat staring at the ground. She was intensely aware of Leon sitting beside her, holding the letter in unsteady hands. At last he folded it carefully and slid it back into the envelope.

"Why?" burst out Laura. "Why did her father stand in their way for so long? Couldn't he see how much she loved him—and how much he loved her? Couldn't he see that he was breaking their hearts?"

"Mr. Visconti was Italian," said Leon. "He was probably Catholic, and I guess her family was Protestant. Like I said, he was different. Different from Veronica's family. Maybe that was why. But her father must have understood a little, at the end. When it was too late."

"When she was dying," said Laura bitterly.

"Maybe then all those other things did not seem so bad anymore. Maybe they didn't matter. Death does that." Leon sounded as though he was speaking about something he understood.

Laura looked at him uncertainly. "What do you think we should do with the letters?"

"I'm not sure."

"I wouldn't want just anyone to read them. Someone who didn't care or who might laugh at them." Laura thought of people like Kylie, Maddy, and Janie.

Leon placed the letters back in the secret drawer. "Maybe one day you should write the story of Mr. Visconti and Veronica," he said. "You could make people understand."

"People made fun of me when I wrote about the garden," replied Laura. "I wouldn't be able to make them understand. I'm not good enough."

Leon shook his head. "That's nonsense. I saw the way people looked at you when you were reading your paragraph. They thought it was great. Of course you can do it."

No one, thought Laura, had ever paid her a greater compliment.

"For the moment, though, I think you should keep

them and look after them. Until you're ready." Leon paused, then added, "I would like to show them to my dad and grandma, if that would be all right."

"Of course," said Laura. "They are yours, too. We found them together. And I want to show my mom and dad and Isabella and Harry. They will understand." She slipped her hand shyly into his. "I wish you didn't have to go. I'm going to miss you so much."

And then Leon did a very surprising thing. He kissed her.

## CHAPTER 28

On the last day of school, two letters arrived in the post. The first was in a small envelope and was addressed to Laura's parents. Laura passed it to her mother with hardly a glance. Her eyes were fixed on the second envelope. It was large and stiff and had a cluster of Italian stamps, covered in heavy black postmarks. Her name was written on it, *Signorina Laura Horton*, in sweeping, elegant letters. Laura was so mesmerized by the package, it was only when her mother shook her that she realized she was being addressed.

"Look at this. It is from the Barlows."

Laura took the letter and ran her eyes over the opening paragraph. Then she breathed in sharply and began to read more closely.

> *Dear Mr. and Mrs. Horton,*
> *Stan and I have been thinking about the*
> *statue in our garden. Now that we know more*

*about Mr. Visconti and his story, we feel that the statue should be returned to the garden from which it came. It does not seem right to have it separated from Mr. Visconti, but with the vandalism that is around these days, we do not feel it would be safe to leave it in the graveyard. It would be terrible to find it broken or damaged. If you would be happy to have the statue, we can arrange for our son to bring it over in his truck. We greatly enjoyed meeting you and finding out more about the history of our house. It has certainly made us see the old place in a new light. The children have done a wonderful job in uncovering the story.*
*Looking forward to hearing from you.*
*With all best wishes,*
*Doris and Stan Barlow*

"I can't believe it," exclaimed Laura. "It's so wonderful. It will be like Veronica is finally coming home to her house." She looked up at her mother. "It's strange; I thought they didn't understand at all. Just like I thought Miss McInnes didn't understand. But they did. They all understood in their own way."

"People understand things differently. And

express how they feel differently, too. It's one of those things you learn after a while." Her mother smiled at her. "I must make them something to say thank you. Something suitable," she added, catching Laura's eye. "So what is that other package?"

Laura looked back at her large, flat envelope. "It's from Italy," she replied, turning it over. "I think it's from Mr. Visconti's family."

"Well, aren't you going to open it?"

Laura shook her head. "Leon will be here soon. I'll wait for him."

She carried the envelope off to her room and sat cross-legged on her bed, staring at it. What could be in it? Could it possibly be the paintings? She held the parcel up to the light but nothing was visible through the thick buff-colored paper. Nothing moved when she shook it. She bit her lip, trying not to get too excited. Maybe somebody was just writing to say that they had not heard of Mr. Visconti. But if so, why would they send such a big envelope?

Laura studied every mark and every crease on the package while she was waiting for Leon. Her imagination was fermenting with ideas about what might be in it. The second she heard his knock, she grabbed the envelope and headed to the door.

"So much has happened, Leon," she cried. "I thought you were never going to get here. The Barlows want the statue to come back to our garden. They wrote to Mom and Dad about it. The letter arrived today." She paused for effect. "And so did this." She thrust the large envelope under his nose. "It has come from Italy!"

Leon's eyes widened and he took it from her, holding the envelope as though it wasn't quite real. "They answered our letter."

"Yes. And they've *sent* something. Can you believe it? They've *sent* something." Laura tugged at his arm, shaking him with excitement.

"We should open it in the tree house," said Leon. "Come on."

They dashed from the kitchen, across the yard, and out into the orchard, all green now with its summer foliage. Once they had scrambled up the ladder and were settled on the rough floor, Laura began to pry open the flap of the envelope. She drew out a letter and two pieces of cardboard, stuck together with tape.

"Which should we open first?" she asked, looking at Leon. Laura felt as though they were both suddenly very close to Mr. Visconti.

"The letter," said Leon.

She unfolded it carefully. The paper was thin, and at the top, there was the familiar crest. Leon slid closer, and together they began to read.

> *Dear Signorina Horton,*
> *Thank you for your so interesting letter. It is a long time since my grandfather, Gabriele Visconti, died but I remember him to have spoken of his cousin who went to Australia and never returned. I did not before know why. I have looked through his papers and I have, indeed, found the paintings of which you wrote. I am sending them as my grandfather would have wanted. I would be most grateful if you would send a photo of the house which Carlo Visconti built.*
> *Distinguished greetings,*
> *Gabriella Visconti*

They looked at each other and Laura took a deep breath. Leon's eyes were dancing.

"They *did* send the paintings," said Laura.

"Yes. It's unbelievable. Hurry up. Open the package."

Laura peeled off the tape and there, between the two pieces of cardboard, were five small watercolor paintings. The first was of the house, as seen from the gates, grand and gray, with storm clouds behind it. The second was of the garden, full of sunshine and flowers, with the monkey puzzle tree and the palm still quite small. Then there was a painting of the conservatory, shady with ferns.

"Imagine how exotic all these plants must have been," said Leon. "How different from Italy."

"And how hopeful Mr. Visconti must have felt, planting it all for Veronica."

They turned to the next sheet, and there was the ballroom in all its grandeur, waiting to come alive. A huge chandelier hung from the ceiling, and the windows were thrown open to show the roses growing outside. There were elegant chairs lined along one wall.

The ballroom was magnificent, but it was the last painting that really took Laura's breath away. This was of the room with the murals. The trees and the steps and the statuary were all there, fresh and bright under soft skies. It was an exquisite place. A tiny piece of Italy transplanted to Australia. And there on one side was a grand piano, waiting for Veronica, and on the other by the window, a painted chair, waiting for Mr. Visconti.

"He must have loved her so very, very much," whispered Laura, her voice quavering. "Can't you imagine him, sitting there alone in his garden with his heart breaking?"

Leon put his arm around her. "Maybe he didn't feel alone. Maybe he sat in the room because he felt close to her there."

Laura leaned back against him, studying the picture. "And he *did* know that she loved him. That's important, isn't it?"

Leon nodded. They sat for a while, silently, thinking about it all.

"Do you remember that first day when Grandma told us about Mr. Visconti?" said Leon at last. "It seems like such a long time ago, doesn't it? Mr. Visconti was just a name then, a strange, mysterious name. Now I feel like I really know him."

Laura nodded. "So do I. And I really like him."

Leon grinned at her. "You were so uncomfortable that day."

"I wasn't!"

"Yes, you were. You hadn't wanted me to walk with you at all. You couldn't wait to get away. And I was angry. Angry with everyone and everything." His grin changed to a reminiscent smile. "So much has changed, hasn't it?"

"And it feels as though somehow it has all happened because of Mr. Visconti," replied Laura, gazing out though the curtain of leaves. "We would never have come to this town if it hadn't been for his house. And I would never have gotten to know you if your grandma hadn't told us about him."

Leon ran his hand over a knot in the floorboard. "And I would have gone on being angry and lonely. I would have refused the scholarship and hurt Dad even more." He looked at Laura. "We had such an awful argument just before I came to stay with her. He said I had to go, and I didn't want to leave him. We shouted and said terrible things and then we stopped talking. I hated that the most. But Mr. Visconti gave us something to talk about again. Mr. Visconti and you and your family. It was a beginning, and now things are getting better. Dad's job is going well and he has found an apartment." Leon smiled again. "He said we should make a painted garden in it, like Mr. Visconti, because the apartment is small and has no garden outside."

Laura looked up at him. "You know, Mr. Visconti

gave me something else, too. He made me feel it was OK to be different."

"All interesting people are different." Leon twisted one of her curls back behind her ear. "It's one of the things that makes them interesting."

Laura blushed. "You won't forget me, will you, when you move to your big new school?"

Leon raised one eyebrow. "What do you think?"

"Well, there'll be lots of students there. Girls . . ."

"But they won't be you. Like you said, you're different." He put his arm back around her. "I'll be counting the days until the holidays."

Laura snuggled against him. "So will I."

When they took the paintings inside, Laura's father was standing in the kitchen, holding the phone. He had a strange look on his face.

"That was Hugo," he said before they could say anything. "Come into the studio. I have something amazing to tell you all."

They trooped across the hall, and Laura's father made them all sit down before he made his announcement.

"Hugo was right," he said. "I didn't really believe it but the wine *is* valuable. Much more valuable than we realized. We should have enough money now to fix up the house and do a little traveling besides!"

"No!" exclaimed Laura's mother, leaping up. Laura's father swept her into his arms, and they started waltzing around the ballroom together, twirling in and out between the blocks of stone. Laura and Leon burst out laughing, and when her parents finally collapsed onto the sofa, Laura showed them the letter and the paintings.

"He was a man of many talents, your Mr. Visconti," said Laura's mother, examining the watercolors. "And he must have moved in a very creative world, with his friends all singing and painting and making things. Look at how grand this ballroom used to be." She turned to Laura. "It was very generous of Gabriella Visconti to send these to you. We must send her a very special letter to thank her."

Laura, who had been kneeling on the floor beside the sofa, suddenly bounced up. She caught her father by the lapel of his old jacket. "You said we might be able to do a little traveling. Maybe we could visit Gabriella Visconti. Maybe we could show her the letters and photos and all that we have found." She turned to her mother. "You know how I said that when the statue comes back here, it will be like Veronica coming home. Well, taking the letters to show Gabriella would be a little like Mr. Visconti going home, wouldn't it? Like everything going full circle."

Laura's father looked across at her mother. "You know that might be a possibility, Lesley. You always said you wanted to see Italy."

"Would Leon be able to come, too?" asked Laura eagerly.

Leon looked horrified, shaking his head at her, but Laura's mother just laughed.

"We can't make any promises. We'll have to wait and see what happens, but it is a wonderful idea. And if we do go, Leon should definitely come, too." She smiled at him. "The discovery belongs to you, too, you know."

Leon flushed and looked down at his shoes.

"And in the meantime," said Laura's father, "we should have some cake to celebrate. Excitement always makes me hungry, and after this much excitement, I'm starving."

As they all made their way back to the kitchen, Laura turned to look down the hall to the entrance area and the uncovered cellar. For a moment, in the shadows, she saw the figure of an old man. He inclined his head toward her and smiled. The memory of the first time she had seen the house flashed into her mind. She had thought then that it was enchanted, and she had been right. It was.

## FROM THE AUTHOR

My family will tell you that I have an extremely unreliable memory and that I see what I want to see, not what is really in front of me. I have been known to swear that there was an old fountain in a garden when, in reality, there was only a clothesline. I had replaced the clothesline in my mind with the image of a wonderful gray stone fountain, covered in moss and dry grass. Such memory transformations are now referred to by my family as "fountain moments" and, while they may be frustrating at times, are extremely helpful in storytelling. *The Visconti House* sprang from just such a moment.

Driving through central Victoria, we stopped in Inglewood to stretch our legs. I wandered off and came across an old house that captured my imagination. I found myself weaving a story around it. Later, when I saw a photo of the house, I realized I had transformed it from an old Victorian mansion into an Italianate villa, but by that time, I already had Mr. Visconti *tap, tap, tapping* his way through my thoughts and the shadow of Veronica Mackenzie falling across the garden. I had the whole Italian background worked out. It was about this time that Laura Horton moved into my mind and started exploring the house. And as soon as Laura arrived, so did Leon Murphy, and I knew exactly what I wanted to write.

As Mr. Visconti's house became more focused, I realized that two other houses had influenced its creation. One was a tall gray house on a hill in Hamilton, Victoria. In my memory, it was in the Italianate style and overlooked the town, but this may be another "fountain moment." The other was a house near where I grew up. It was a very grand house built by the chain-store proprietor Oliver Gilpin in the 1940s. By the time I knew it, however, it was a convent, and on festival days we children would go to explore it, marveling in the strange network of canals that ran through the garden and the vacant pens, bordered by stone fences, that had once housed exotic animals in a private zoo. We were told that the house had been built for a woman but that she never lived in it. I don't know if this is true, but the story continued to haunt me, and I never passed the house without thinking of it.

So it is from these three houses that the Visconti house and its bittersweet history emerged.

## ACKNOWLEDGMENTS

I would like to thank L. M. Montgomery for filling my childhood with dreams, Sandra Kipp for sharing my love of writing, Christine DePoortere for seeing possibilities in my story, Sarah Foster for offering me the chance to put it into print, and Meredith Tate and the team at Walker Books for guiding me so perceptively through to publication. My love and gratitude, as always, go to my husband and children, who have believed in me wholeheartedly. They make everything worthwhile.